A Kahale and Claude Mystery

#3

OPERATION VARSITY BLUES

Timothy R. Baldwin

Indies United Publishing House, LLC

INDIES UNITED
PUBLISHING HOUSE

Also by Timothy R. Baldwin

Adult Fiction
A Shot at Mercy (2019, 2021)
A Crock of Sundries, Volume 1 (2021)
Chemical Burns (2022)
The Unwanted Guest and Other Short Thrillers (2024)

A Kahale and Claude Mystery Series
Book 1: Camp Lenape (2019)
Book 2: Shadows of Doubt (2020)
Book 2.5: A Bazaar Christmas (2020)
Book 3: Operation Varsity Blues (2020)

Nonfiction
Boy Tales of Childhood Discussion and Writing Unit Plan (2024)

These and more at
https://www.indiesunited.net/timothy-baldwin

For my students, past and present.

Chapter One

Marcus

We sat in Alissa's car in the far corner of a parking lot belonging to a closed down shopping plaza outside of town. Off the beaten path and late at night, we doubted anyone would check on us. A light snow and rain mixture began to fall, which caused a sparkle in the wintery mix. A single streetlamp cast an eerie glow.

From the backseat, Janice shivered.

"Can you turn the car back on?" she asked. "It's cold."

"Here," Nate said as he pulled her closer to him. "Is this better?"

"Not really," Janice mumbled. "But I'll take what I can get until Lis cranks up the heat."

"Okay," Alissa huffed. "I'll turn the car on... again!" She keyed the ignition and looked to me while she shifted in the driver's seat. "Marc, you know I love you, but I'm beginning to think this new contact is playing you."

"He said he'll be here," I said. I pulled out the envelope I'd found in my school locker. "Let's wait another fifteen minutes, and then we'll go."

"I'm all for this, too," said Janice as she leaned forward between Alissa and me. "But how do you know our new client is a *he*?"

"That's no biggie," said Nate as he joined the conversation. "Wait! I see lights ahead."

As the rain continued to fall, a car pulled into the parking lot. Its headlights blinked twice. That was the signal. My heart raced.

"Guys!" I cheered. "We're doing this!"

As the car approached, it looked strangely familiar.

"I don't want to be a buzzkill," Nate said. "But isn't that your dad's car?"

"Sure, looks like it," Janice replied. Meanwhile, Alissa nodded.

"It is," she said.

I groaned as my family's familiar old station wagon pulled up next to us.

Dad left the engine running as he climbed out the car. Dressed in a long, dark trench coat and a black fedora, he stood there with arms crossed.

"What's with your dad's getup?" Alissa asked as she opened the door.

"I think it's pretty cool," Nate said.

The four of us exchanged looks and I sighed.

"Guess we better see what he wants," I said. I

slammed my door shut and trudged over to Dad. "Why are you here?"

The others joined me and expressed a similar sentiment.

Crossing his arms, Dad *tsked*.

"Now, is that any way to treat a new client?" he asked.

"No way!" Nate and Janice exclaimed in unison.

"He's joking," said Alissa as she stepped to me. "Marc, please tell me he's joking."

"I don't think he is," I said regretfully as I continued to look to Dad.

I clicked my teeth. Before my friends and I got here, we hung at my house and then we went to Slices on the Avenue. Dad had time to call us for a get-together then, so I couldn't figure out why he waited until now.

Dad's air of mystery seemed to diminish as he looked from the others to me.

"I...uh..." he stammered. "Here's the thing. I didn't want to get your mother involved, and this is a sensitive subject."

"Can we maybe talk in your car, Mr. Kahale?" asked Alissa. "We're all a little cold out here, and we're getting wet."

Dad climbed into the front seat of the station wagon. Nate and Janice climbed into the back. At the passenger side, Alissa and I hesitated.

"Do you want to sit in the front?" I asked.

"No, I'll take the back," Alissa said as she grinned. "He is your contact after all."

She climbed in the backseat while I took the front. As I closed the door, I welcomed the warmth of the car. Dad took off his fedora and stretched.

"It's a school night, so I'll try to make this quick," he said. From an inside pocket of his trench coat, he pulled out a folded sheet of paper and handed it to me. "There's been an unusually high number of our students getting accepted into prestigious schools despite the schools' extremely low acceptance rates."

I unfolded the slip of paper and glanced at a list of names with corresponding GPAs. I passed the paper to Alissa.

"Normally I would celebrate," Dad continued. "Most of these students are all around good kids, but they don't exactly shine academically or demonstrate the qualities top schools look for in exceptional candidates for enrollment."

"I know some of these kids," said Nate as he leaned forward. "Why not go to Principal Moss with this info?"

Dad sighed. "In our last faculty meeting, he held them up as prime examples of why our staff should continue to push every single one of our students. I did some more digging and discovered a similar trend in years past. Fourteen percent of our students are getting into prestigious schools. That's twice as high as the national average."

"So, why us?" Janice asked. "Couldn't you talk to the superintendent?"

"I could, but given the recent financial scandal—"

"I get it," Alissa cut him off. "Some of the kids still whisper among themselves about your involvement."

"Which is why I bring the case to you," Dad said. "You know your classmates. Pick a handful off this list I gave you that might be willing to talk."

"Or those we can get to slip up," I chimed in.

Dad glared at me. "This isn't something to joke about, son." He shifted his gaze to the back seat. "I wouldn't ask if I had another option."

"This feels borderline illegal," said Alissa as she passed the list to Janice.

"Right," agreed Dad. He cleared his throat. "Which is why I emphasize you don't do anything illegal. You're gathering information. Nothing more. Burn the list once you've picked a handful of classmates. Whatever you find, you bring to me."

"Got it boss," Nate said.

"Thanks, Dad," I added.

"Yeah, thanks for bringing this to us," Alissa said. She paused. "This means a lot."

Dad adjusted his seat. "If you have any doubt about this, you're under no obligation to follow through, okay? Now, get back home before ten o'clock. It's a school night."

We returned to Alissa's warm car as Dad's station wagon drove off. In the backseat, Janice waved around the slip of paper.

"This is so exciting, you guys!" she cheered. "We got a case, and I think I know who each of us should start with."

While Janice and Nate discussed the list, I glanced at Alissa. She remained silent. I had a feeling she wanted out, which would leave Nate, Janice, and me to do this on our own.

Chapter Two

Alissa

As I tried to review my notes for the upcoming A.P. Statistics test on Monday, the after-lunch chatter in the classroom distracted me, and my mind cluttered with thoughts about this case. I glanced to my classmate and teammate Mel's empty seat. She played on the soccer team with me as a senior. Though her name wasn't on the list Mr. Kahale gave to us, I knew she was tight with a few of the girls, and I wanted to ask her some questions. Flustered, Mel rushed into the classroom, dropped her books on her desk and sat. At nearly six feet tall, she towered over all the girls and most of the boys. She turned to me and grinned.

"You're not going to believe this!" she exclaimed.

"What's that?" I asked.

She eagerly handed me an envelope.

Immediately, I recognized the crest of Penamore College — dual roaring lions emblazoned in gold, matching lettering, and a red background.

"See that, Lis," Mel said. "I got into my dream school!"

"Oh," I stated.

Mel laughed. "Don't look so surprised."

I shrugged in a lame attempt to laugh it off. "I'm not surprised. Mel, this is incredible!"

"I know, right? They even offered me an incredible scholarship program." She leaned toward me. "Lis, you should apply next year. Between your grades and soccer, I bet you'll get in. They have a great law program. Plus, for the sports scholarship, you really should go out for lacrosse this year. With three of us from the same team, we'd be unstoppable."

"Who's the third?" I asked.

She rolled her eyes. "Abby, of course. Our team was so lost without her last year."

Because of her failing twelfth grade, I wanted to say. Instead, I grinned. "That'll be awesome. Maybe you, me, and Abby could practice this weekend."

Mel slid her acceptance letter away. "Uh, sure. We could do that. But it'll have to be way early. She—"

"Good afternoon, class," Ms. Berry, our statistics teacher, called out as she entered from the back of the room and brought Mel's explanation to a halt. "If you haven't done so, take out your homework."

Our papers shuffled as Ms. Berry pulled up her presentation for the day. She reminded us of our big test on Monday. I, on the other hand, wondered what else Mel and Abby had planned for Saturday.

Then, I recalled two months ago after we —

Marcus, Janice, Nate, and I — solved the case surrounding the missing school funds. Janice had handed me her phone. On one of her many social media apps, I saw Abby Jenkins posing while wearing a Penamore College t-shirt. Her caption read:

They said I couldn't do it. I don't even like school. Hi, haters. Look where I'm going.

Janice and Nate were convinced we had a potential case. Marcus and I wondered how Abby could've gotten into an exclusive school like Penamore. But we didn't have a legit reason to pry, not if we wanted to keep what little popularity we'd managed to earn. Then Mr. Kahale brought us the list last night. Abby was on the list.

What previous doubts I had about getting involved in this case vanished. With Mel's acceptance into the same school, I needed to figure out a way to get close to Abby. I thought Mel could help and be the person to find out more about Abby. If Janice joined the lacrosse team with me, that would help, too.

"Alissa!" Ms. Berry called, which pulled me from my thoughts. "Please read question four."

"Uh, okay," I said in a daze. I glanced at my paper and read aloud. "You run an office that employs 23 people. What is the probability that two of your employees have the same birthday? For the purposes of this problem, ignore February 29."

I paused. "Oh...can you get back to me? I know the answer. I just need a minute."

"Take all the time you need," Ms. Berry said. "Let's go on to the next problem as Ms. Claude gathers her thoughts."

I ignored the giggles and whispers because now the thoughts of Penamore College and Abby Jenkins' apparent acceptance returned. Maybe with Abby being a second-year senior, the college somehow accepted her on probation. But that seemed doubtful. Her grades sucked. Plus, the odds of getting into a school like Penamore had to be extremely low. Even lower for two students from the same high school.

A nudge at my shoulder jolted me back to AP Statistics.

"Fifty Percent!" I shouted. "That's it!" Glancing around, I realized the room was silent. Everyone stared at me, including Ms. Berry. She glared for a moment before she grinned.

"Very good, Ms. Claude," she replied. "Do you care to explain?"

"I'd rather not." Now, I only had room for one statistical problem.

Ms. Berry frowned for a moment. While she proceeded with an explanation, a new angle for our investigation into Abby Jenkins began to form in my mind.

The bell rang.

"Drat!" Ms. Berry exclaimed. "All right, class. You've got two nights to study. You're—"

The shuffling of feet and scraping of chairs interrupted Ms. Berry's farewell. In the hallway, I caught up with Mel.

"Hey, can Janice come with us this weekend?" I asked her.

"I didn't know Janice was into sports," Mel said. "We could definitely use another middie and you're a shoo-in for attack."

"That's awesome! Do you think Saturday morning at ten would be cool?"

Mel's face flushed. "I'll have to check with Abs. You know, she might want to take the day to get ready for Saturday's party."

"Right, I almost forgot." I lied. "I was going to bring Marcus."

Mel cocked her head. "Okay, just that Abby's boyfriend Derrick isn't even coming."

"Oh..." I paused as I tried to play off Mel's dismissal. "I'll have to reread the invite. I didn't think this was a girl only party."

Mel fumbled with her books. "Don't sweat it. Boys are allowed. I need to get to class, so I'll let you know about getting together to practice. Even if we can't, I'm sure you and...uh... Janice will pick up the game fast. Okay, see ya!"

She turned and disappeared into a group of students. At the end of the soccer season, she bugged me about playing lacrosse in the spring.

"Girl, you are so out of it today!" Janice squealed as she walked up to me.

"You don't know the half of it," I said as I turned to her. With a grin, I changed my tone. "How about we crash Abby's party this Saturday?"

Janice's eyes lit up. "I thought you'd never ask. I heard some chatter about it. It sounds super exclusive, so if we do get in, we'll have to stay under the radar."

That evening we met at Marcus's house.

"Are you sure you kids don't want any snacks?" Mrs. Kahale asked.

"You four look like you've got a lot of studying to do," said Mr. Kahale.

"We do," Marcus answered. "If we're not done in an hour, I'll come down and bring something up for my friends."

"Thanks, Mrs. Kahale," I said. Janice and Nate thanked Mrs. Kahale, too, and the four of us headed upstairs.

With one earbud in her ear, Marcus' sixth-grade little sister Bri met us by her door.

"Hey, Lis," she said. "Oh, you're all here! Do you have a case? Can I help?"

"I don't know," I said as I teased Bri. "You have to ask Marcus." I looked to Marcus and he blushed.

"No, Bri, you can't help," Marcus blurted. "We aren't on a case."

"We're doing a...school project," Nate lied.

"You all are terrible liars," said Bri as she rolled her eyes. "Just keep it down because I have studying to do." She popped in her earbud and slammed her door shut.

"Real smooth, boys," Janice said.

"What?" Marcus asked. "I couldn't find a more covert place to meet, so my parents' house is what we got."

After closing the door, we all took a seat. I filled the boys in on my theory of the statistical impossibility of two people from a small town, like ours, getting into a school like Penamore.

"So, I'm thinking you two could do some research into that," I said. "Maybe check with Ms. Calhoun, our guidance counselor."

"That's a great idea," Marcus said. He turned to

Nate. "You and I could come up with a list of leading questions, right?"

Nate nodded and exchanged a look with Janice. He opened his mouth to speak but hesitated. Although they only remained quiet for a moment, I sensed something was up with Nate and Janice.

"Am I missing something?" Marcus asked. "I know it's not all glamorous, but we need to keep things going."

"I'm cool with that," Nate said.

"Well speaking of glamorous, Abby's got a party this weekend," I said. "I think Mel can get us in. Janice and I are supposed to meet with them Saturday morning."

"Since when?" Janice asked.

I turned to Janice. "I may have nominated you for lacrosse this season, and we'll need a working plan for getting into the party."

"Definitely," Nate said. "Why are we attending?"

"We need to get close to our subjects," Marcus replied. "I'm sure a handful of people from the list will be at the party."

I nodded. "Yeah, I've seen some of them hang with Abby. Others will probably be there, too."

Janice added. "And clues. I'm sure we could go through a few drawers in the house."

"Just remember," I said. "We need to keep this clean and legal."

Later, we'd work out a line of questioning for Ms. Calhoun and some scenarios for getting ourselves into Abby's party. I wondered whether there was a way to legally acquire clues. I doubted anything would be so obvious, like a falsified grade report, especially since none of us had ever been to Abby's house, nor knew exactly what we were looking for. We would have to figure it out when we got there.

Chapter Three

Marcus

Friday afternoon found me at stage one of our investigation. Alone, I paced the hallway outside the guidance office. In a distant corridor, a single locker slammed. Except for the locker door, the building was eerily quiet. No teachers roamed the building or socialized in the hallways. I glanced at the list of questions we'd put together yesterday evening. Nate should've been here five minutes ago.

A rhythmic click of shoes on linoleum flooring drew my attention in another direction. Rounding the corner, Principal Moss skimmed a handful of papers as he marched my way, barely registering my presence. When he looked up, we made eye contact. He forced a smile.

"Marcus," he said, "you're here late, but you're probably getting a ride with your father."

"That's right," I said as I stuffed my hands into my pockets. "Where is he?"

"Faculty meeting. I'm surprised you didn't hear the announcement." Nate skidded to a halt behind Moss, who turned to greet him. "I should've known. You guys seem to come in pairs. Or in fours." He glanced down another hallway.

"Hey, Principal Moss," said Nate as he shifted his feet. "We're here to—"

"Get some work we left behind," I interjected. With Moss's back to me, I shook my head to Nate. Moss took a step back.

"Go ahead, and make it quick," Moss said. "I'll see you boys later."

As he raced off to the media center, Moss's oversized blazer flapped behind him.

With Nate and I alone, he came closer to me.

"What was that about?" Nate asked. "It's like he popped out of nowhere."

"I know," I said. "I wouldn't worry about that, though. Should we go over our notes again?"

Nate ran his fingers through his hair. "I'm good. But there's just something you don't know...about me, I mean."

Though there were few people I knew better than Nate, I waited him out. After glancing around, he stepped closer to me.

"I never told you this, but I failed most of my core classes freshman year," he said. "That's why I never bothered with sports."

Suddenly, last night's silent exchange between Nate and Janice made sense.

"I guess Janice knows," I said.

"She does," Nate said. "She already knew about

my parents' divorce. She didn't know about my grades that year."

I clapped him on the shoulder. "I get it. You had other things to worry about."

He smiled weakly. "Right, other things. I wanted you to know about my academic records. I'm sure Ms. Calhoun will bring them up."

"We can play that to our advantage," I said. "We'll use your freshman scenario with low grades and tell Ms. Calhoun you're failing now."

Nate cringed. "Obvious much? That'll be the only time I'm ever compared to Abby Jenkins."

"Believe me, it'll be between you and me. You ready?"

We bypassed the secretary to head into the counseling office. Being the son of an administrator at the school had its perks, like no wait times or need to schedule appointments, but I didn't want to take advantage of the perks right now. Dad took on the role of assistant principal this past semester after the financial scandal went down. He told me don't draw unwanted attention to him, my friends, or myself.

Since the light was on and her door was open, I stepped into Ms. Calhoun's office. When Ms. Calhoun noticed us, she flinched. Standing, she pulled a stack of papers into her arms. She glanced between Nate and me.

"You're early and I see you've brought a friend," said Ms. Calhoun.

"I hope that's okay," I said. "You know Nate."

She nodded. "Of course. I've seen you two together. Give me a second while I organize this paperwork. Why don't you two take a seat?"

I sat while Nate pulled up a seat beside me. Ms. Calhoun seemed to search for a space on her shelves to place her papers. She settled on stacking them on top of another pile. Turning, she flattened out the wrinkles in her skirt and gave us a smile.

"I'll get to that later," she said. "Now, Marcus, you're starting your school search, right? I've got your records pulled up. Nathan, do you want to do the same?"

"That's right," Nate said.

"Excellent," replied Ms. Calhoun. She placed her fingers over her keyboard. "Just give me your last name. I'm still getting to know everyone here." After giving her his last name, Ms. Calhoun tapped on her keyboard. "I'm assuming you two are okay with sharing each other's academic records."

Nate sat up. "Of course. We know everything about each other already."

Ms. Calhoun looked at her screen, using her mouse to toggle between our files. "In that case...you both have a pretty good academic record. Though...Nathan, your freshman year wasn't so hot."

"I know. I was wondering how colleges would see that."

Ms. Calhoun squinted at her screen and did a few clicks. "That's an understandable concern. Given your current academic record, I don't think you need to worry about that. You're consistently carrying A's and B's. A high school transcript tells a story. But an admissions counselor will look at your high school career holistically. They're human, so they'll understand you went through a transition your freshman year."

She, of course, didn't know the half of it. Neither would an admissions counselor. Still, I wondered.

"What if someone were going through some sort of transition that impacted their records during their junior or senior year?" I asked. While Ms. Calhoun stared at her screen, she tapped at her keyboard for so long I began to wonder if she was writing notes.

"That's a... funny question," she replied slowly. She forced a laugh. "Marcus, you don't need to worry about that at all. And, Nathan, unless you're planning to sabotage your high school career these next three semesters..."

"Nope," Nate said as he placed his hands on the desk. "We just want to make sure we aren't missing anything... still, hypothetically speaking—"

"We don't need to speak in hypotheticals," Ms. Calhoun interrupted him.

In one swift motion, she clicked at her keyboard and swiveled in her chair as her printer whirred to life. She grabbed some papers, turned back to us, and handed each of us a copy.

"Here's your current grade reports," she said. "You two don't need to worry about anything. You both have outstanding academic records. Even you, Nathan, managed to recover well since your freshman year."

Nate shifted in his seat. "What if, I don't know, I took all A.P. courses next year? And I do sort of well my first semester, then completely bomb my final semester."

Ms. Calhoun narrowed her eyes. "Like I said. Let's not speak in hypotheticals. But I don't think it's wise to intentionally sabotage your senior year after getting accepted into a school."

Nate shifted in his seat as he examined his report. "So, your grades do matter, even in your final semester?"

Ms. Calhoun nodded. "Of course. We send the final transcript at the end of the senior year. A school admissions counselor, even at a state school, will definitely want a good reason for poor grades at the end of your senior year."

Nate sat up. "Glad that's settled."

"Oh, I almost forgot." Ms. Calhoun clasped her hands together. "Nathan, you may want to consider getting involved in something extracurricular. Are you going to the athletics meeting on Tuesday?"

"Actually, we were planning on going together," I said.

Nate glared at me for a moment. If Ms. Calhoun noticed Nate's reaction, she didn't let on.

"That's a good start, boys," she said. "And you can figure out which activity you want to do after the meeting."

Nate cleared his throat. "Yeah, uh, I'm really looking forward to hearing everyone's spiel about why I should join."

Ms. Calhoun smiled. "Also, you both should keep in mind that it's a lot more difficult to get an A in an A.P. course. You both would do well to challenge yourselves academically next year, especially since you're closing out your career pathways. I'd recommend you add one extra A.P. course to your load next year."

Ms. Calhoun handed us course enrollment forms for the fall. "Think it over. Talk with your parents. It'll do you both some good." She stood. "Now, I've got some work to finish up before I go. Feel free to schedule your next meeting with the counseling secretary."

After thanking her, Nate and I left. When we were safely outside of the building, we stopped. I pulled out my phone.

"What do you think?" I asked.

He looked over his enrollment sheet. "I really want to know how Abby could repeat senior year and still get accepted in a school like Penamore. Even with everything Ms. Calhoun said, it doesn't sound likely."

"Not unless they loaded their senior year with A.P. courses and aced every single course."

Nate sighed. "Who knows? Good thing we have that list."

"We should probably go and destroy that list soon." I headed toward the exit and Nate followed. "Now, let's talk sports. We could use a sprinter in track and field."

"See, Lis," said a familiar, perky voice from behind us. "I told you Marc would convince him."

Nate and I turned to see Janice grinning. Alissa stood beside her, with eyes rolling.

"I never doubted you for a second," she said.

"To be clear," Nate said, "I didn't agree to anything."

"Oh, come on," whined Janice. She sidled up beside Nate. "Don't be such a downer."

I laughed as Nate and Janice fussed with each other. Alissa approached and I gave her a quick kiss. Then, Nate and I gave a recap to the girls about how colleges viewed academic records.

"Well, whether it's all true or just rumors," said

Janice. "I think we should celebrate across the street with pizza and pop."

"I don't see why not," said Alissa. She slipped her arm in mine. "Let's go."

As the four of us crossed over to the shopping center, I worried. In this small town, rumors spread. Which meant the rumors would spread even more in our little community at Lenape High. It would be hard enough to sift through the rumors and discover what Abby Jenkins was about. Maybe Abby's acceptance into Penamore was just that, a rumor. Either way, we had to tread carefully. We didn't want people to figure out we were "those meddling kids" too soon. If they did, then the case Dad assigned us would be dead before it even started. Somehow, tomorrow's party needed to reveal something, that is, if we could even get in.

Chapter Four

Alissa

In the gymnasium on Saturday morning, Janice and I were on our tenth rotation of suicides when Mel finally entered with a lacrosse stick.

"Sorry, I'm late," Mel said. "You two seem all warmed up."

"Oh, good!" Janice heaved. "I'm glad you're here, Mel. I thought Lis here would drill me until I was literally dead."

Mel laughed. "Janice, you act like you've never played a sport with Alissa."

Janice deflated a little. "I have. Just nothing serious, that's all."

"Well, girl," I said, "we're getting serious right now."

"It looks like you two could use some sticks," Mel said. She pointed to a corner in the gym.

"Coach usually keeps extra equipment in the closet, so look back there. I'll be warming up."

While Mel did some leg raises, I surveyed the gym. A small group of people began a pick-up game of basketball while others ran the track around the gymnasium. But I noticed someone was missing.

"Is Abby coming?" I asked.

"No, she really had a lot to do," Mel said as she stopped her exercise "So, it's just us three, which will be better, I think."

"Why's that?" Janice asked.

"Abby's really good at lacrosse, but she's not that patient." Mel grinned and picked up one of her sticks. "Now, how about those sticks?"

"Right, how could we forget?" Janice rolled her eyes in my direction.

Janice and I jogged toward the corner of the gymnasium. Once there, I opened the closet door and peeked inside. Janice followed me inside and switched on the lights. An array of used equipment from basketballs to football shoulder pads lined the shelves. In a basket, I spotted some lacrosse sticks.

"Well, here we go," I said as I grabbed two of the sticks.

"Any idea how to use this?" asked Janice as she took the stick and twirled it.

"Sort of. Mel thinks we can both pick up the game pretty quick."

"Well, that takes care of lacrosse, but it still doesn't get us into the party tonight."

I sighed and smiled. "Let's wing it, shall we?"

After switching the lights off, we met Mel at the

center of the gymnasium.

"Okay," she said. "Looks like you've gotten the boys' sticks. But it'll be okay for now."

Mel demonstrated how to hold a stick — dominant hand in the middle, non-dominant hand at the bottom of the stick, so both hands were about shoulder width apart.

"I can remember that," I said. Looking at Janice, I could tell she seemed to have it as well.

"Great," Mel said. "Try this. I like to call this the triple threat position." As she cradled her stick, guiding the head through her legs and around the world, Janice and I followed her lead. "Don't forget to breathe," Mel reminded us.

As I let out a breath, Janice bit her lower lip and seemed to drag the head of the stick through the air.

"Janice, put some of your theatre experience to work," Mel said. "You're a dancer, right? Pretend it's a dance. Relax your shoulders and let the stick do the work for you."

Following Mel's instruction, Janice's stick seemed to glide through the air.

"I think I got it," Janice said. "You're a great teacher!"

"Thanks," Mel said. "Abby wasn't so sure about you two. If we get to the party early enough, you might be able to show off your new skills!"

"Oh..." Janice's voice trailed off as she looked to me.

"So, about tonight's party," I said. I glanced expectantly between Janice and Mel.

"Don't worry," Mel said. "I know you weren't invited. But I've got your back. Janice can come, too. We're a team, right?"

"Great!" I exclaimed.

"Okay, now that you two are invited, let's do some passing."

We put some distance between each other and created a triangle. Mel passed the ball first to me and then to Janice. Both of us missed and overthrew the ball several times. Even though Mel seemed cool, I wondered about her. When I lied to her about going to tonight's party, she seemed unbothered, even now.

"Nice catch, Janice!" Mel called, which pulled me away from my thoughts. "Alissa, I knew you'd pick this up quick. But, Janice, once you relaxed, you had it."

"Thanks," Janice said. "I don't know why I didn't pick this up earlier."

"Pass it back!" Mel held out her stick while Janice launched the ball, landing it perfectly in Mel's netting.

"Nice one!" I yelled. I crouched and readied my stick to catch it.

"Nah, girl," Mel said. "I think you're ready to run. Go to your right!"

Like in soccer, I tracked the ball. As I came close, I held out my stick and let it land in the net.

"All right, let's bring it in!" Mel cheered.

"Mel, thanks for everything," I said. "And, um, sorry about lying to you about being invited to the party."

"It's no problem," Mel said. "It's just a party. Besides, everyone in the school wants to go, so I got you in. Feel free to bring your plus ones."

Mel gathered her things while Janice and I

returned the sticks we borrowed.

"What do you think?" Janice asked. "Can we trust Mel?"

"I think so," I said. "But we definitely can't trust her with the details of our investigation."

As we said our goodbyes, I still had to wonder how Mel remained so calm and cool, especially knowing I'd lied to her. If she had even a shred of motive for or against us, I'd be watching for it tonight.

The bass downstairs pounded out the latest K-pop songs. Waiting for Janice, I stood outside the upstairs master bedroom. I leaned against the door and knocked.

"Janice, hurry up," I said. "You've been in there long enough."

I peeked around the corner to see a few kids headed downstairs, with red solo cups in hand. No, they were not filled with booze. Marcus shot me a thumbs up. He was our lookout, hanging in the living room with Nate just in case. Not having been to Abby's house prior to this night, that was our hastily put-together plan. When we met Mel outside Abby's house an hour ago, she warmly greeted us. No one gave us a second glance, not even the hostess Abby Jenkins. Still, I kept a watchful eye in the hallway, just in case Abby, or even Mel, caught onto what we were doing. Though I knew Mel well, she still seemed way too cordial.

The door I leaned against cracked open. I took a step forward and turned when Janice peeked out.

"Are we all clear?"

"Yeah," I replied. "What took you so long?"

She stepped out. "I had to be thorough. Besides, their closets are, like, the size of my bedroom."

I sucked my teeth. "Okay, but did you find anything?"

Janice shook her head. "Do you get the feeling that Mel is up to something?"

"I don't know, but we'll have to guard ourselves around her."

"That's an understatement," Janice said. She pointed to a pink door. "This has gotta be Abby's room." She gently touched the door, which popped open. "Wish me luck."

Janice shot me one last grin before she closed the door and left me to wait once again in the hallway. The soft-white glow of her tactical pen's flashlight illuminated the cracks within the doorframe. Marcus insisted the team carry a tactical pen wherever we went, especially on missions, so I had mine now. I had to admit, it did come in handy. On the other side of the door, I heard Janice, rustling through closets and drawers. While she snooped, I stayed as her accomplice. I hoped we were well within our limits of legal.

I placed my back against the pink door to what we assumed to be Abby's room and knocked.

"Janice, are you done?" I asked.

No answer. I wasn't sure she heard me over the Korean hip-hop blasting through the house. A light swept across the doorway and shifted its glow to what I imagined to be another side of the room. She was taking way longer than she did in the master bedroom. I would've thought she planned to swipe some of Abby's Cartier bracelets, but we had a code. No theft and no breaking and entering (anymore). Snooping and creating mayhem when needed was okay…I guess.

From downstairs, I heard Mel laughing.

"Abby, where are you going?" she asked. "The party's down here."

"Girl," Abby said, "I'll be back, but I need to go upstairs."

The stairs creaked as she ascended the steps.

I froze. Marcus hadn't given us the signal. In any other situation, I'd dip in a sec.

My eyes darted from doorway to doorway as Abby's footsteps came closer. I grabbed the handle to the bathroom next to her bedroom.

"Excuse me," Abby said as she crossed her arms. "What are you doing up here?"

Abby wore black eyeliner and way too much blush. Although she was one of the shorter girls in school, she didn't let her height define her. She had an attitude, and I felt like it was about to be a girl fight if I couldn't give an explanation.

"Sorry, I was looking for the bathroom," I lied. I gave her a once-over and smiled faintly. "Cute outfit, though."

Abby laughed. "You can stop with the fake compliments." She pointed to my outfit. "I can tell someone helped you pick clothes because you don't usually dress like that. Where is she?"

I gulped. Abby could tell I was up to something. I needed Janice, but I didn't know how much longer she would be.

"Sorry, Abby," Mel said as she joined us at the top of the stairwell. "They needed to use the bathroom."

The bathroom door popped open, and surprisingly Janice emerged with tears in her eyes.

"Crap!" she shouted. "Someone bumped me downstairs, and now I can't get out this stain out of my blouse. I knew I shouldn't have worn white." She wiped her eyes and looked to Abby. "Can I borrow your clothes?"

"Is that it?" Abby asked. "Don't cry over that. I've got plenty of blouses. Why don't you take that off and give it to me?" Abby held out her hand.

Janice and I exchanged a glance. She shrugged, slipped off her blouse, and handed it to Abby.

"Can I borrow anything?" Janice asked.

"Yeah, just don't take anything on the left side of the closet," Abby said.

As Janice flipped the light on and rummaged through the closet, I waited for her. I leaned against the wall, observing Mel and Abby, who sighed.

"Seriously, you could've just said they were up here," Abby said. "I suppose you invited them."

"Yeah, I did," replied Mel. She blushed. "Sorry, I didn't think to tell you."

Abby shrugged. "Hey, what's a party without a few extra guests?"

The door popped open. Janice, wearing a lacy, red blouse, spun once.

"What do you think?" she asked.

"It looks fabulous on you," said Abby as she

went to Janice to touch the fabric. "Keep it if you want."

Janice squealed. "Really? I mean…thanks."

Abby tossed the soiled blouse into the bathroom. "Was there anything else you needed while you were up here?"

I chewed my inner lip. Janice seemed to be at as much of a loss for words as myself.

"Hey, Abs, I think they're good," Mel spoke. "Let's all—"

A crash came from downstairs.

"Oh, no," Abby whispered. "I hope that's not what I think it is."

As Abby dashed down the steps, we followed at a safe distance in case she suddenly stopped at the bottom of the steps. In the living room, a small crowd formed a circle.

"I leave you all alone for one second!" Abby shouted above the clang of the electronica music, now blasting from the speakers. A few people turned, and then I spotted the glass scattered across an oriental rug. I rubbed my temples. Someone on our team changed the plan.

Abby darted toward the glass.

"Who did this?" she asked. "My mom's gonna kill me!"

"It was an accident," someone said. I heard the bass in the voice and recognized the person as Marcus. He moved from the crowd while Abby took a step toward him.

"I can't believe someone invited you," she said. Then, she pointed at Janice and me. "And I still don't get why you two made the cut. Seriously, no more open invitations if all ya'll gonna take liberties."

"Hey, what'd I miss?" asked Nate as he joined Marcus. After spotting the broken glass and the stupid looks on our faces, Nate looked to Abby. "You know if you need to be reimbursed, my family can—"

"Thanks, but no," Abby interjected. She laughed. "It's just a Waterford."

Nate's eyes grew wide. "Well, whatever it is sounds expensive."

Abby shrugged. "For some." She directed her attention to the circle. "Now, somebody's gotta get this cleaned up. Then, we can really party."

A couple of kids from school scurried away and quickly returned with brooms, like they did this type of clean up before. I attempted to help with my friends, but Abby halted us.

"Nope, you four can leave," said Abby.

"But what about your blouse?" asked Janice. "I can wash it and give it back to you."

Abby smirked. "Consider it a gift. I was going to get rid of it anyway." Abby waved dismissively. "See you at school or whatever. I'll let Mel walk you all out since you're her guests."

As Marcus and Nate joined Janice and me, I couldn't help but think one thing. Abby and I had nothing in common. I shook my head while Mel opened the front door for us.

"Sorry you guys have to leave so early," said Mel.

"Not a problem," I said. "Thanks for inviting us despite everything."

"Anytime," Mel said. "See ya at school. If you want to practice some more, let me know."

While Mel returned to the party, we headed to our cars. Marcus and I walked entwined in each other's arm. Nate hugged Janice to his side.

Once we were at a safe distance from Abby's house, Janice spoke up and moved from Nate's embrace.

"You guys!" she shouted. "I don't know if this means anything, but I took this pic while I was snooping around."

"Let me see," I said. I took the phone and expanded the image. "Is this an acceptance letter from cosmetology school?"

"I wouldn't be surprised," Marcus harrumphed. "Cosmetology seems to suit her; with the way she's done up and..." His voice trailed off.

"Oh, please continue," I said sarcastically. "I just love the way you compliment Abby."

Marcus nudged me. "Don't be jealous. I was just saying Abby does goes heavy on the make-up sometimes."

"Well, okay, lovebirds," said Janice as she swiped her phone from me. "There's more. Look at this."

She flashed us two photos: a rejection letter from Penamore College from less than a year ago and an acceptance letter from last October.

Nate stroked his goatee. "Ms. Calhoun did mention the holistic nature of college acceptance. But I can't imagine the same school rejecting and then accepting someone that quickly."

"Well, I think this was a good start," Marcus said.

"Yeah, more clues have gotta be coming our way," Janice added.

We fist bumped and parted ways to our own vehicles.

As Marcus joined me in my car, I gave him a wink.

"Shall I take the lead on this next part, then?" I asked.

"It's all yours, babe," Marcus said.

We leaned across our seats to give each other a kiss. I couldn't imagine life any better than this. A new case coming together, an amazing friend now boyfriend, plus acing all my honors classes. I felt like my hard work was making a difference.

As for my peers, like Mel and Abby, I felt like they were doing the opposite—easy work that paid off. I couldn't understand. Regarding honors classes I knew Abby Jenkins never took any. We were missing something.

"Marcus," I whispered, "I need you and Nate to dig up more about Abby's academic record."

"Okay, I'll see what Nate and I can find," Marcus said. He rubbed the back of his neck. "We should probably tell my dad about what we found today."

"I'll let you take the lead," I said.

When I pulled into my driveway, Mr. Kahale and another shorter, stockier man were talking on the front steps of the Kahale's house. Vapors of breath passed between them in the cold air.

"Who's that with your father?" I asked.

"No idea," Marcus said.

The two men shook hands. Mr. Kahale waved when he saw us. The other man descended the steps. I tracked him in the rearview mirror until he arrived at a dark sedan where the lights flashed once before he opened the driver side door.

"That was weird," I mused.

"Yeah," Marcus said as he got out of the car and opened my driver's side.

I got out of the car and grabbed my bags from the backseat as Mr. Kahale strode over to us.

"How'd the party go?" he asked, as if he wasn't just talking to some mystery man in the shadows.

Marcus took a deep breath before he explained our findings: the acceptance/rejection letters, the broken Waterford, and Mel's apparent help. Mr. Kahale studied us for a moment.

"Her parents weren't around, were they?" Mr. Kahale asked.

"We didn't see them," I said.

"And don't worry about the broken vase," Marcus added. "Abby said it was no big thing."

"We'll let time determine that," Mr. Kahale said. "On your findings, her first rejection makes sense. The two acceptance letters, even the one from cosmetology school, sound fishy."

"Is there anything we can do?" Marcus asked.

"You two have done a lot so far." Mr. Kahale scratched the stubble on his cheek with a faraway look in his eyes. "For now, keep your head down, your ear to the ground, and see what else you can find out."

I shot a glance at Marcus, waiting for his cue.

"Is that it?" he asked.

"That's it," Mr. Kahale said. "Now, don't stay up too late." He turned and walked toward his house next door.

Once Mr. Kahale secured himself inside the

house, I backhanded Marcus on the shoulder. "Why didn't you ask him about that man?" I asked.

"You could've asked him," Marcus retorted.

I crossed my arms. "He's your father."

Marcus laughed. "You got me there. I'm going to do some research tonight and maybe ask my dad another time about the mystery man."

"You better," I said, clutching his jacket as I took a step toward him. "But we did good tonight, right?"

"Totally." Marcus gave me a quick kiss.

After wishing each other a good night and gathering up our things, we parted toward our respective houses. As I entered the warmth of my house, I imagined Marcus asking his father about the mystery man. But I knew he wouldn't. His mind was too busy occupying itself with plans for snooping around his father's office. I wondered what his father knew that he wasn't sharing with us.

Chapter Five

Marcus

"What're you guys working on now?" asked Bri from the back seat of Alissa's car.

"Nothing much," said Alissa, giving me a sideways glance as she continued to drive.

Bri and I used to ride with Dad, but not anymore. Ever since he took the role of assistant principal, he had to get to Lenape High far too early to drop off Bri at the middle school.

"Here's your stop," said Alissa.

We pulled into the middle school.

"You never told me about your plan," said Bri. She rolled her eyes. "I'll just have to guess." As the car came to a stop, she let the seatbelt fly, causing it to clank on the side paneling.

"Hey, watch it." I said as I turned to Bri in the back seat.

Bri hopped out the car. "You two are the lamest high schoolers I've ever met. Check your Instagram. Oh, wait, you're never on it. Bye!" She slammed the door.

"What's gotten into her?" Alissa asked.

"Who knows," I said.

As Alissa left the parking lot, Bri skipped toward the barren entrance of the middle school. She was at least thirty minutes too early to school.

"Do you remember when Bri and I used to be buds?" Alissa asked. "It seems so long ago."

"Yeah," I agreed. "Once you and I made things official, it's like things changed between you two."

Alissa sighed. "Change is inevitable. I guess... what's on Instagram? I'm surprised Janice and Nate haven't heard anything."

"We'll find out soon enough," I said.

We passed a cluster of trees as Alissa pulled down the access road leading to the school parking lot. When the school came into view, the lot swarmed with activity as upperclassmen darted out of their cars almost as soon as they parked them.

"Why do I feel like we're late?" I asked.

"I think we're okay," Alissa said. "There's still plenty of people out front."

We got out, grabbed our bags, and headed toward a small cluster of students. Nate and Janice emerged from one cluster, running toward us.

"You're not going to believe this!" Janice shouted.

Nate shot a look over his shoulder at the crowd. Several sets of eyes seemed to lock onto us.

"It's not good," Nate said.

"Check it out," said Janice. She handed her phone over. "I can't believe you never check your social media."

"I check it sometimes," Alissa said defensively as she took Janice's phone.

I sidled up beside her to get a better look. A montage played on the screen. Immediately, I recognized scenes from Abby's party on Saturday: Nate flailing his arms and legs wildly. Someone behind him knocking the crystal vase over. Caption: Party Busters. A cut to Abby walking down the steps with Alissa, and Janice right behind her. Caption: *Watch out for girls who steal your favorite blouse when you're not looking.*

"No way!" Alissa shouted. "That's not the way it went down." Alissa returned the phone to Janice and directed her attention to the crowd. "Mel!" She called out.

While Alissa shook her head about the false Instagram post, I spotted Mel, a tall blonde with a tan, in the crowd. I waved to her. She looked our way, shook her head, and seemed to dissolve back into the crowd.

The bell rang.

"Looks like our buddy Mel just gave me the cold shoulder," I said.

"It's been like this all morning," Janice said.

"Or all of five minutes." Nate said.

"Well," Alissa said, "looks like it's going to be an interesting day."

Alissa marched toward the dissipating crowd as it funneled into the school building.

We joined our fellow classmates in the hallowed halls of Lenape High where rumors ran rampant and the truth appeared hard to find.

At the start of first period, whispers surrounded me.

Can you believe them?

Who crashes Abby Jenkins's party?

Not me, that's for sure.

The tips of my ears seemed to burn as I made a poor attempt to bury myself in a search for my homework. It didn't help that the desk to my right shifted away from me as a handful of classmates continued their gossip under their breaths.

As our teacher Mr. Cifra entered, the class came to order. He launched right into directions.

"Your reading notes should be out," he said. "As you know from last class, we'll be discussing Edgar Allan Poe."

Pacing the classroom as he lectured, he momentarily hovered over each desk to check work and move on. When he returned to the front of the class, he turned to face us.

"You have thirty seconds to shift your chairs and break into small groups for today's discussion on mood and setting for The Fall of the House of Usher," he said.

Metal legs scrapped across linoleum flooring as my classmates cloistered themselves into tight, little groups. Seeing one group close to me still maneuvering their seats, I slid my desk through a rapidly closing hole and sat.

"Now that you're all settled," said Mr. Cifra as he surveyed the room, "I'll designate the group leaders." He dropped a stack of papers on my desk, making me the de facto leader of my group.

Three sets of eyes seemed to bore into me as I took my copy off the top and slid the rest of the stack to my right.

Krista, the recipient of the papers, stared at them through thick framed glasses before she pushed them away.

"I can't believe I have to work with you, the party crasher."

"Yeah," Trae, the tall and athletically built classmate, added. "Derrick told me you guys just broke in."

"Derrick wasn't even there," I said as I leaned forward. "Besides, Mel invited us."

I scoffed in disbelief that Trae doubted me. While Trae and I weren't friends, we got along well-enough. Trae, being on the cross-country team with me, sometimes sat with my friends and me during lunch. I had a feeling that wouldn't happen today.

"Trae, don't listen to him," said Rayna, another one of my group members. "Marcus says he was invited, but I doubt he got one of these." She pulled out a pink striped envelope. "This is Abby's official invite." Rayna slipped the envelope back in her binder.

As I stared at the envelope on display in Rayna's hand, I wondered whether my friends had to deal with the same pressure as me right now.

Krista took a paper and handed the rest to her

right. When the others received a paper, I read the first question and waited a whole minute before my group members said anything. Compared to my group, the rest of the groups appeared to have lively off-topic discussion. When Mr. Cifra passed other groups, they cleverly shifted their conversation back toward mood or setting. I would've preferred that to the overwhelming silence from my three classmates staring back at me.

The classroom intercom beeped, causing the class to fall silent. "Please send Marcus Kahale to the office," said the secretary through the intercom.

"On his way," Mr. Cifra said.

I gathered my things as quickly as I could. For the first time ever, I was thankful for being called to the office. The moment I left; the classroom erupted with chatter. Somehow, Alissa, Janice, Nate and I had the worst luck after this past weekend. I rejected the idea this had anything to do with Janice finding those letters from the colleges in Abby's room. No one knew what we were up to.

Chapter Six

Marcus

The phrase "dead man walking" crossed my mind as I trekked the barren hallways and lively classrooms. I glanced inside one of the classrooms. Someone returned my glance with either a scowl or a jeer. The teacher took a few steps toward the door and slammed it shut. Echoes reverberated off the lockers.

As I rounded the last corner, I spotted Alissa through the glass windows of the main office. She slouched in a chair and pressed an ice pack on her eye. Across from her sat another girl, with arms crossed and a scowl directed to Alissa. Janice and Nate, unusually subdued, sat to Alissa's right. As I entered the office, I saw Janice's eyes wet with tears and Nate's stone-cold expression boring a hole through the desk of the lead secretary Mrs.

Heinemann. Mrs. Heinemann looked up.

"Have a seat, Marcus, while I make a call," she said. She picked up her phone. "Principal Moss, they're all here." Placing the receiver down, she directed her next comment toward us. "He'll be with you in a moment."

Dad emerged from the main hallway as I took a seat. Wide-eyed, he came over to us and sat.

"What have you four gotten into?" he asked frantically. "I saw the footage. I thought the party went well."

"It did, but I guess we were wrong," grumbled Alissa.

"Mr. Kahale," said Principal Moss as he entered the archway, leading toward the administration offices. He peered at us through squared framed glasses. "I'll see them now."

We all stood, but Moss shook his head. He smiled pleasantly at the other girl in the office and gestured to her.

"Mr. Kahale, please assist this young lady," said Principal Moss. "I'm going to have a little chat with the others."

Dad nodded and clasped a hand on my shoulder.

"Catch up with you four later," said Dad. He turned to Alissa. "When you're finished with Principal Moss, I'll need to talk to you as well."

Dad directed the other girl to sit while we followed Moss. My shoulders tensed. I imagined Alissa, Nate, and Janice felt pretty much the same as me. When we came to Moss's door, he stood by it, with one hand stuck in his pocket.

"Please do come in and have a seat," he replied.

Once we were seated, Moss closed the door behind us and sat on his side of the desk.

"Are we in trouble?" I asked.

Pinching the bridge of his nose, Moss took a deep breath, let it out, and looked up.

"I don't know if I told you, but you four were a tremendous help last semester," Moss said. "But you also caused a few more problems than were necessary." He pointed a finger at each of us. "You need to tell me. What is it you're up to?"

"Are you saying we had something to do with the video being passed around?" asked Alissa.

Moss cleared his throat. "I'm not saying that at all. It's probably just a silly prank. But one that was likely provoked."

The burning in my ears returned.

"We don't know who made that video," Janice said. "But I don't think it'll be that hard to guess." She smiled, but her smile faded when she noticed Nate shot her a sharp look. "Not that we know who did it."

"Well, when you find out, please let me know," said Moss. He leaned back. "Clever kids, like you four have your ways. But don't think I'm not keeping an eye on you." He handed each of us a pass, which we took without a thank you.

Once we passed through the front office, we convened in the hallway. Alissa still held her ice pack over her eye. She winced as she turned to us.

"I'll have to hang back here," she said. "Maybe we catch up during lunch."

"What happened to your eye?" I asked.

Alissa removed the ice pack and placed both hands on her hips as she looked at me. "Me and this other girl got into it over that video. She hit me with a ball right to the face. I think we should lay low for a while. Let's regroup when this video thing blows over."

I winced at the sight of her swollen eye. If only I were there, I would have tried to stop the drama. I exchanged a look with Nate, just so I could avoid staring at Alissa's one eye.

"Hey, Nate, I saw the vid!" shouted a scruffy junior. "Nice one!" He laughed when he spotted the rest of us. "You all were good, too!"

"Thanks, bro, I guess," Nate said as he waved.

While Nate basked in his newfound popularity, I scratched my head. I waited for the junior student to pass.

"What was that about?" I asked.

"Beats me," said Nate. "I've been getting shoutouts all morning."

"Lis and Marc, you two seem to be getting the brunt of things," whispered Janice. "No one's booed Nate and me."

"We need to find out who made that video," Alissa said. "I think I know just the right person to ask."

With our next move at play, we parted ways. I hoped Moss would squash this thing with the video. Otherwise, we'd have to take drastic measures. I wasn't so sure we were equipped to handle that. In the meantime, I knew what I needed to do.

Chapter Seven

Alissa

Mel stayed close to Abby's side as two other girls in Abby's posse sashayed alongside them down the crowded hallway. I maintained a safe distance behind them and watched as a crowd of ninth graders parted before the girls. I glanced at one boy who stared too long at these girls that he tripped. When he saw I caught him, he pulled his books toward his chest and ran off, eyes focused on the floor in front of him. The ninth-grade hallway, a terrible design the school administration talked about fixing one day, was in our direct path to lunch.

A bell rang out a warning to straggling ninth graders as I approached the cafeteria. There were several entrances, all of which the girls had already passed. I hoped Mel would hit the cafeteria line while Abby, who never ate lunch, and the other girl would go through another entrance. Chatting and laughing, the four of them continued toward the lunch line together.

A quick nudge to my right caused me to stop and turn. Janice grinned and started to walk with me.

"Girl, how'd it go with Mr. Kahale?" she asked.

"He gave me after-school detention for disrupting class," I said. As Abby, Mel, and the other two girls disappeared around the corner, I picked up my pace.

Janice walked faster. "I'd feel sorry for you, but you're definitely in a hurry. Are you doing some recon?"

"Yeah, something like that." I looked to her. "I was trying to catch Mel before our next class. Do you think you could create a distraction?"

"Are there any limitations on that distraction?" Janice wiggled her eyebrows. "You know I'm with the drama."

For a moment, I pondered how Janice could help without doing too much. She tended to be theatrical, which was good in her drama classes, but I needed her to be discreet here.

"How about you follow my lead?" I asked. I pointed to the cafeteria entrance. "You go through here while I try to catch up with them in line. When you hear me say, 'Girl', that's your signal to create a distraction."

Janice gave me a thumbs up as she headed to the lunch line exit. Meanwhile, I picked up my pace to catch up to Abby, Mel, and the other girl. At the end of a long line of upperclassmen, I tip-toed and leaned away from the wall, trying to catch a glimpse of Mel's blonde hair. I spotted her some twenty students ahead as she disappeared into the salad line.

Good choice, I thought.

Most of the other students went through the line for today's special, which usually amounted to dry, brown, and pasty. When I finally entered, Mel and the others were five students ahead of me. They continued to chat and laugh, but between the clanking and scraping of lunch line activity, I couldn't tell what they were saying. Suddenly, Mel turned toward me.

She flashed me a smile and a wave until she noticed Abby's stoic expression. Abby whispered into Mel's ear, and then they eyed me. The line moved. Abby and Mel made their way to the condiments table just outside the lunch line. One of the girls with them paid for her lunch and moved on. I searched frantically for Janice. A boy fumbled with some change in his pocket. Abby and Mel moved on. I spotted Janice, so I decided to do the signal now.

"Hey, Mel!" I called out. "Girl! I've been trying to catch up with you all day."

Mel and Abby turned. Just behind them, Janice made her move. She positioned herself between the girls and started a conversation with Abby. While Mel fidgeted, I punched my student ID into the keypad and approached her in line.

"Thanks for waiting up," I said. "Can I ask you something?"

"Sure," Mel answered nervously. She nodded toward Abby. "Make it quick, though."

"You don't remember seeing all those phones out at the party, do you?"

She averted her eyes. "I was, you know, kind of distracted, so no."

"What happened after the party? When we left, I mean."

"You seriously want to get into it here?" She glanced around the cafeteria. I realized the kids at the tables closest to us had stopped eating.

I lowered my voice. "I guess not, but—"

"Listen," Mel interrupted me. "Something's come up. You really should stop."

I felt small as she stood over me and pulled her tray closer to her chest. Abby joined us and gave me a once-over.

"What do you want, Alissa?" Abby asked me.

"It's nothing," Mel said. "Lis was just asking about how to join the lacrosse team."

Abby paused. "All right, let's go, Mel. Our lunch table's filling up."

When they left, and I scratched my head. I looked to Janice. Her face appeared pink. They played us. Mel covered for me, but now I could tell she knew something. I took a swig from the water bottle precariously placcd on my tray between my chicken Caesar salad and an oatmeal cookie.

"Hey, Lis, are you okay?" asked Janice as she stepped in front of me. "Let's sit by the boys."

"Yeah, sure," I said. I spotted Marcus and Nate at our table. "I'm good. Mel and Abby just...how'd it go with the distraction?"

Janice winked. "Swimmingly. I told Abby I'd be seeing her at the first lacrosse meeting tomorrow."

"Did she take you seriously?"

Janice cocked her head. "What do you think?"

I laughed. "I want to hear all about. But first, can we sit and eat? I'm starving."

As we skirted to our table, I saw Abby and two others in her posse, eyeing us, except for Mel. She kept her head down, picking at her salad, not even pretending to avoid looking my way.

When Janice and I arrived at our table, Marcus and Nate were fixated on a cell phone propped up between them. We sat our trays on the tables and plopped down. Neither Nate nor Marcus looked up. Janice and I exchanged a look. She snatched the phone.

"Hey," Nate said. "You can't just take that."

"Oh, look," said Janice as she showed me the phone screen. "Someone decided to join the twenty-first century."

"What do you mean?" I asked.

Janice handed me the phone. I stared at the screen for a second until I realized Marcus had reopened his Instagram account.

"I can't believe this stuff on there," Marcus said. "Nate showed me these hashtags. We've been exploring them. You know, looking for the first account to post the video."

"Did you find anything?" Janice asked as she crossed her arms on the table.

"Sort of," Nate said. "It's a little tricky because there's over a hundred accounts that posted and at least three different versions of the hashtag."

"Let's see them," I said.

"Look up username laxislife362," Marcus said.

"There's just the one video."

I smiled weakly. "I'm glad you all found something. I just wish you would've told me sooner."

Marcus did a face palm. "I'm such an idiot. I was so excited that I didn't think you'd mind."

"Don't worry about it. Tell me what you guys found."

"Click on one of the hashtags," Nate said.

When I clicked the hashtag, a few accounts associated with the hashtag showed up.

"Is that it?" I asked.

Marcus nodded. "We can do some more digging later."

"That'll work. Now that you all have told us what you've learned, I think it's time Janice and I share our little recon."

We explained our suspicions about Mel to the boys. Marcus and Nate oozed enthusiasm.

"This case is really coming together," Nate said. "What's next?"

As we speculated on the prospects of checking on more of our classmates, the bell rang. Although we made some progress, somehow, I needed to get Mel to talk to me next class.

Chapter Eight

Alissa

As we filed into A.P. Statistics with Ms. Berry, I heard a comment or two about the video posted on Instagram.

Okay, I need to get back on my account, I thought.

I still had a few minutes before Ms. Berry was due to arrive, so I clicked on the app store.

"Listen, I'm really sorry," said Mel as she took her seat beside me.

"For what?" I asked. I glanced at my phone to check whether my app finished installing.

She cringed. "Someone sent the video to my phone and I shared it."

I swiveled toward her. "Do you know who made it? Who sent it to you? Who is laxislife362?"

Mel shrank in her seat as the classroom went

silent. "Not so loud."

I pretended to study with my notebook open. Our classmates resumed their usual chatter. Mel leaned toward me.

"Do you want to know a secret?" she asked.

"Go ahead," I replied. I pushed my notebook to the side. "It's not like I need to study today's test."

Mel looked around the room to make sure no one was watching us. "Did you know Abby's entire family, including her older brother, went to Penamore College?"

"Huh?" I shook my head. "Wait, how...what are—"

"Good afternoon, class!" Ms. Berry called out. "Big test today! Put all materials, except for a pencil on the floor beneath your seats."

Today marked the second time Ms. Berry barely made it to class on time. If this happened a third time, rumors would spread.

While Ms. Berry passed out the tests, my classmates and I shuffled our things to clear our desks. When she placed my test on my desk, I stared at it for a moment. When Ms. Berry gave us the go, I breezed through one statistical problem after another. But my head wasn't clear.

Mr. Kahale had given us this case for a reason. While I've known Marcus's family all my life, I didn't know everything that happened with them at home or at school. Marcus wasn't aware either. Last semester proved that. Still, I wondered if Mr. Kahale knew about Abby's family. The statistical likelihood of siblings getting into the same prestigious school seemed slim, especially when one of the siblings didn't have the grades to support admittance into the school. An intercom rang.

"Teachers," said the secretary over the intercom, "please turn on your televisions for an important announcement from our principal, Mr. Moss."

"Drat!" Ms. Berry exclaimed. "Why do they always interrupt in the middle of my class?" She set down her materials and began fumbling with the television. "If this takes long, you'll just be taking the test tomorrow."

I made a mental note to ask Mr. Kahale about Abby's brother, and then I joined the rest of the class in ignoring Ms. Berry.

"What's the deal with Abby's family?" I asked Mel.

"So," Mel said. "You didn't hear this from me, but Abby wanted to go to cosmetology school. I think she applied to one of the top ten schools."

"Why would she apply there?"

Mel shrugged. "I think she did it to spite her family. I've been friends with her since elementary school."

I gasped. "I had no idea!"

"Class, please quiet down," Ms. Berry said. "Principal Moss is speaking on the TV.".

I suddenly became aware of the drone of his voice on the intercom.

"Let me remind you," said Moss. "Cyberbullying will not be tolerated in this school. I suggest you all look at your phones right now. If you have any comments, videos, or photos that put your classmates down in any way, you delete them. I'll wait while that is taken care of."

I stared at the television screen, knowing full I didn't have any part in the cyberbullying. I peeked at the rest of my classmates. No one else, including Mel, reached for their phones. Everyone seemed to stare ahead, like they didn't have their phones or any idea of the video of my friends and me.

"Thank you for taking this time," Moss continued. "Once again, I'm sure your classmates will appreciate this gesture."

A few snickers rippled throughout the room, which didn't surprise me.

Ms. Berry shut off the television. As soon as she was about to speak, the bell rang for class dismissal. While my classmates exited the room, I rushed to catch Mel in the hallway.

"Is there anything else you can tell me?" I asked her. "What about the Instagram account?"

"You might want to talk to Derrick, Abby's boyfriend," Mel said.

"But why him?" I flailed my arms. "He wasn't even at the party."

Mel fumbled with her books. "I don't want to be late for class, so maybe we can talk later. I'm glad you and Janice will be at lacrosse."

Mel walked away and blended into the crowd of students. Before today, I felt anxious, but my shoulders relaxed as I thought about the little lead I gained. Now that I knew Derrick's possible involvement in the case, I thought about how to reach him.

"Hey, there, detective," joked a familiar voice.

I looked behind me, and Marcus approached with Nate and Janice. The boys seemed to be in a good mood, which I hoped would make them more open to the task I had planned.

"Marc and Nate," I said as I faced my friends. "I need you two to do something for me."

"I bet it's some recon," Janice whispered to Nate. "Case work is the only time I've seen Lis get this excited."

"I heard that," I said playfully to her. "And you're right. I do have a new lead in the case. It's Derrick, Abby's boyfriend, and I need Marc and Nate to talk to him."

"Oh, no, not that guy," whined Nate. "He's a douche."

I crossed my arms. "Maybe you just haven't gotten to know him. Either way, I need you to talk to him. Mel dropped a hint that he may know something about the Instagram account laxislife362."

"Mel sure does know a lot," Marcus said. "I'm surprised she told you all this."

"Me, too," I said. The bell rang. "I'll figure out a plan by lunch time. I'll catch you all later."

Janice and I left the boys standing in the hallway. As we walked, I thought about what Marcus said. Mel seemed to know more than I thought, which made me suspicious. Somehow, we needed to get her to tell us everything she knew.

Chapter Nine

Marcus

Nate and I reached the locker room just as the late bell rang, giving us less than five minutes to change. Hurrying through the corridor into the locker room, we heard laughter. With a knowing glance at each other, Nate and I paused.

"Moss is a joke if he thinks that announcement will stop us," said one of the boys.

"Yeah, but that video posted," Derrick said. "Whoever laxlife362 is, I can't wait to see what he posts next."

Suddenly, their laughter and their chatter ceased. Someone let out an uncomfortable laugh. Nate and I entered as we made our way to our lockers.

"Hey guys," Nate said. "Don't mind us."

"Anyone know what we're playing today?" I

asked.

"It's C-Pass and B-Pass," said Derrick.

I smirked. "Great. Did you wanna play me?" I popped open my locker and grabbed my uniform.

Derrick laughed. "I'll crush you."

"Warm-ups in two minutes!" yelled the teacher. "Quit your yakking and get out here!"

The other boys headed out while Nate and I continued to change into our gym clothes.

"How is challenging Derrick going to get us any answers?" asked Nate as he pulled on his shorts.

"Not sure," I said. I shoved my feet into my shoes and sat. "Guys like that respect skills, and I'm competitive."

"Hey, guys," said a squeaky voice.

We looked over and noticed Justin, a scrawny classmate of ours who wore sports goggles to PE class. I wondered how much of the conversation he heard.

"When'd you get here?" I asked.

"Sorry, I was... it doesn't matter," said Justin. "I just wanted to say you better have a lot of skills if you're planning on going against Derrick."

Nate and I waited for Justin to further explain, but he didn't. Instead, Justin darted out the door.

"What's his deal?" Nate asked.

"Remind me to add Justin to our list of people to question," I replied as I laced up my shoes.

We exited the locker room and joined the rest of the class in the usual warm-up routine: jumping jacks, stretching, and suicides. If our teacher noticed our lateness, he didn't show it. But Derrick noticed. He made it a point to pass closer to me as we sprinted from one side of the basketball court to the other. Somehow, he'd challenged me to a game of chicken. I couldn't think of any other motivating factors except for his general air of cockiness.

The gymnasium echoed with the pounding of rubber on hardwood. Basketballs bounced and sneakers squeaked. Nate, lazily bouncing a ball, stood beside me. Two kids, one from the front of our line and one from the front of our opposing line, raced each other around an obstacle course. They did chest passes at higher targets or bounce passes at lower targets set up around the gymnasium. The hoop was at the end of the obstacle course. A line of students waited beneath the hoop. They were ready for a quick game of one-on-one when the runner on the course arrived. The boy from our line went for a layup, which the opposing team easily blocked. The boy from the other line took his turn.

"Derrick is eighth in line," Nate said. "You should trade places with someone so you can get his attention to challenge him."

I stepped out of line. By this time, I had to find the seventh person in line.

"Looks like that would be Justin," I said. "Maybe you can do some questioning while I go against Derrick."

"I'm on it," Nate said. I stepped out of line. From across the gymnasium, I managed to catch Derrick's attention as I walked up the line. With a nod, Derrick acknowledged my challenge.

I tapped Justin on the shoulder. He looked up at me, lenses fogging from too much perspiration.

"Hey, Justin, can I trade places with you?" I asked.

"You don't have to ask me twice," Justin said happily. He popped out of the line and joined Nate. Now, I found myself at the front of the line with Trae at the front of the opposing line. He smirked. I'd let him believe I intended to go against him.

The whistle blew. Dribbling and running, I hit the first target with a chest pass while Trae missed. Leaving him behind to do it over, I made it to the next four targets, hit them both, and pivoted toward the hoop.

Derrick took center court, so I faced him. I dribbled while Derrick took up a defensive position. I attempted a fake to my left, but Derrick quickly matched my movement. When I readjusted for a fast break, someone else dribbled beside me. Suddenly, Trae slammed into my side and knocked me to the floor. When I looked up, Trae dunked on me. The whistle blew.

"Trae, take the bench!" hollered our P.E. teacher. "Marcus and Derrick, you two reset."

Derrick reached out his hand. "Tough break. Are you good?"

"Yeah," I said. I took his hand to get up. "Let's play."

After our reset, I dribbled and faked to my left, which caught Derrick off guard. Making a fast break, I plunged forward to the basketball hoop. As I released the ball, Derrick tipped it. Our classmates cheered.

Derrick held out his fist. "Nice moves, bro."

"Thanks," I said as I gave him a fist bump.

"Yours were better, though."

We moved out the way to switch lines.

"I know I've been playing longer than you, but you were good," said Derrick. "I think you should go out for the team. Your boy Nate should try out, too."

I thought about Derrick's suggestion. Although I preferred to stick with track and field, the basketball team would allow me to find out more about Derrick. Nate would be good on the team, too. I watched as he easily outpaced his opponent and completed an uninhibited layup. I turned to Derrick.

"Sure, we'll be there," I said. "We'll see you at signups tomorrow night."

"See ya there," Derrick said. He jogged to the other side of the gymnasium.

"What was that about?" Nate asked.

"Looks like we're trying out for basketball."

Nate groaned. "Do you get the feeling this is way too easy? What if we're being set up?"

I surveyed the room. As Justin passed by, he eyed us quickly before he took his spot in line.

"Did Justin tell you anything?" I asked.

Nate kept his eye on Justin. "He thinks Derrick is out to get us, but I don't know why."

The P.E. teacher blew his whistle, signaling that Nate and I needed to get back in the game.

Back in the locker room, Nate and I overheard a few jeers from Derrick's friends.

"Marcus's game is trash," said one of the guys. "He nearly schooled you."

"That would have been as bad as the video

posted to laxislife362," said another guy.

"Shut up!" Derrick demanded.

"Uh, guys," I said. "We're right here. Besides, Derrick and I were just having some friendly competition." A few of the guys snickered, but they stopped when Nate banged on his locker.

"My stuff's gone!" Nate shouted.

"What the heck?" I asked. I went to his locker and my eyes grew wide. "Who did this?"

Derrick came to our side of the lockers.

"Man, that sucks," said Derrick. "You must've forgotten to lock up." He turned to the rest of the guys in the locker room. "Yo, who's messing with Nate?"

Lockers slammed. Our classmates exited the locker room. I worried we wouldn't find Nate's stuff, but Justin started to wave frantically.

"Hey, Nate," he said, "I think your stuff's in here."

We turned. Justin stood by the trash can, reached in, and pulled out Nate's school clothes and notebooks.

"Oh snap!" Trae called out as he exited while Justin handed Nate his stuff.

"I'm gonna see what Trae knows," Derrick said. "Catch ya tomorrow night." Derrick left, leaving Nate and I standing in the locker room. We began to change.

"Do you really think Trae would mess with my things?" asked Nate.

"Trae seems like the obvious choice," I replied. "I don't remember actually seeing him on the bench after he ran into you."

The bell rang. As we headed to class, my phone

buzzed to indicate a direct message from one of my apps. I would've checked it, but we were running late already.

Chapter Ten

Alissa

I easily spotted Mel in the crowd of students exiting for the day. Her height, of course, gave her the advantage of speed as she moved down the hallway and out the side entrance. When I finally made it out the door, she was already halfway across the parking lot. I thought to call her cell phone but decided against it. At the pace she was moving, a call from me would likely be ignored. Zipping my coat against the cold, I picked up the pace. Alongside me, a car pulled up. I did a double take when I realized it was my own. Marcus rolled down the window and winked.

"What's a beautiful lady like you doing out in the cold?" he asked.

"I'm tailing Mel, silly," I said as I chuckled. I gestured to the farthest corner of the parking where she was headed.

Marcus braked. "That's weird. Her car is parked next to yours as usual, but she walked right past it. I'll give you a lift."

I entered the passenger's side. "It feels weird having someone else drive me in my car."

Marcus shrugged. "It's the least I can do. You've been working hard on this case, like the rest of us."

"Well, thanks, but let's make sure we don't lose sight of Mel. I think she may be meeting someone. I wanted to ask her about Abby's family and who made the video."

Once I fastened myself securely in the passenger seat, Marcus eased on the gas. As we followed Mel, a Lexus sedan pulled up beside her. We stopped. Marcus pulled into the closest parking lot. We couldn't make out anything because of Mel's back, shielding the driver from our view.

Mel shifted nervously while we spied from a distance. She walked from the vehicle, leaving the driver's side momentarily exposed. A dark-haired man with sunglasses glanced out the car window as it rolled up. The car began to pull out the parking lot, so we followed it.

Keeping a safe tailing distance, Marcus backed up the Nissan and followed the Lexus out the parking lot. My heart raced when I pulled my phone out and snapped a quick picture.

"Good call," Marcus said. "We may need to identify the car later."

"Hopefully it's nothing," I said. Still, I sent a quick text, letting Janice know what's up. In the same instant, Marcus's phone buzzed.

"That's funny," I said. "Your phone buzzed at the same time I sent a text to Janice."

Marcus kept his eyes on the road. "Yeah, that is funny."

I expected Marcus to be more interested, but I understood he needed to focus. I placed my phone back in my pocket.

Ahead of us, the Lexus accelerated through a yellow light. Too far behind to get through the light safely, Marcus pumped the brakes until we stopped. We were first in line at the red light.

"This light is taking too long," Marcus mumbled.

Ahead, the Lexus shrank into the distance. Marcus focused on his target while his phone buzzed constantly.

"Aren't you mister popular?" I asked sarcastically. "Who's sending you messages?"

"Some randos on Instagram," Marcus said. "It'll start and then stop."

"And that is why I'll never reactivate my account." My phone chimed, so I checked my new text message. "Looks like Janice saw us in the school parking lot. She and Nate are following Mel."

"Sounds like a plan. I'm gonna turn down this road."

Once the light changed, Marcus sped forward, which pushed me back against my seat. Spinning the wheel, Marcus cut off an oncoming car, causing me to shriek as I grabbed the handle above my door.

"Sorry," Marcus said. "I didn't want to lose our

guy."

"After today, you need to let me drive," I replied. "Please be careful with my car." I took a deep breath and sat up in my seat. I was aware I sounded like my mom when she taught me how to drive, but I didn't care.

Glancing down one side street and then another, we rolled down a narrowing roadway lined with piles of snow and dumpsters.

"What would that guy be doing driving down this alleyway?" Marcus asked.

Behind us, a car beeped. Looking back, I half expected to see the Lexus we'd been following. Instead, I spotted a white Cadillac.

"The real question is who's behind the wheel in that car?"

Marcus glanced in his rearview mirror and whistled. The headlights of the Cadillac flashed once. Marcus pulled down the next side street. The Cadillac followed us. As I chewed my inner cheek, I couldn't help but wonder what we were getting into.

"Don't worry, Lis," Marcus said. "We're good. Whoever's in that car is probably just headed to one of these businesses." When Marcus took another right, the Cadillac followed us.

"There!" I yelled. To our left, I spotted the Lexus in a parking lot marked Genesee Country Club Parking Only.

"Relax," Marcus said. "I'm going to turn down the main street up ahead. Maybe there's visitor parking in front."

I let out a nervous laugh. "Of course."

Behind us, the Cadillac turned into the parking

lot while we hung a left. Once on the main street, there were a few empty spots.

"Think you can handle parallel parking?" I asked.

"Babe," Marcus said, "I can handle anything."

I rolled my eyes. "Okay, well make sure you don't hit the curb."

While Marcus pulled up next to a vehicle, I texted our location to Janice. Looking up, I cringed as Marcus eased the car back into the spot. I popped the handle of my door, which swung open with barely enough room between the bottom of the door and the sidewalk.

"You parked too close," I said as I got out. "I definitely need to take the car keys from you."

"Fine," said Marcus. He held out his hand for me to take it. "You can drive on the way back...maybe."

I wanted to be mad at Marcus, but the country club entrance distracted me. I took his hand and gazed up at a Romanesque three-story brick mansion in the heart of downtown.

"This place is beautiful," I said breathlessly. "Look at all that marble."

"Let's see how we can get in," Marcus said.

Once on the stoop, Marcus tried the door. It was locked. Spotting an intercom to my right, I pressed talk. It buzzed. I hit Marcus playfully. He rolled his eyes.

"Can I help you?" asked a woman over the intercom.

"Uh, hi," I said. Heat rushed to my face. "My name is Alissa and I'm here with Marcus. We're...uh...juniors at Lenape High. We were wondering about employment here."

"Come on in," said the woman.

The door clicked open. Marcus smiled.

"Real smooth," he said.

As we entered, an elegantly dressed middle-aged woman, sitting behind a counter, greeted us.

"Several of our members have children who go to your school," she said. "Is that how you heard about positions?"

"Actually, we couldn't find an employment section on your website, so we decided to arrive in-person," lied Marcus. "We wanted to make a good impression."

I shook my head at Marcus's made-up story while the woman chuckled and picked up a pen and pad of paper.

"That's fine," she said. "I'll just need to verify. We are an exclusive club, after all. Who referred you?"

Beyond an arched doorway leading to one of several rooms connected to the lobby, I spotted the dark-haired man. Marcus nudged my shoulder.

"We overheard there were positions," I added quickly.

"Listen," said the woman. She put down her pen. "To work here, you have to know someone who's a member. That's why you don't see an employment section."

The dark-haired man entered and ignored Marcus. He gave me a quick glance.

"Carol, is there a problem here?" he asked.

"No, Mr. Maddox," Carol replied. "They were just leaving."

"Thanks for your time," I said as I turned to leave.

"Yeah," Marcus said flatly. "We really appreciate your help."

Mr. Maddox nodded at us briefly while Carol buzzed the lobby door.

Taking our cue, Marcus and I exited quickly. Once we were safely in the car, Marcus and I turned toward each other.

"That was close," Marcus said.

"Yeah, it was too close, like your parking," I replied.

Marcus winced. "Ouch. You didn't have to go there."

I shrugged. "I'm just speaking the truth."

As we laughed, I looked behind us. Carol and Mr. Maddox watched us from the front entrance of the lobby. I quickly turned around and moved faster.

Marcus keyed the ignition, eased on the gas, and pulled out of the parking spot.

"What's Mel's connection to Mr. Maddox and the Genesee Country Club?" I asked.

"Whatever it is," Marcus said, "maybe she can get us in."

"Yeah." My phone chimed. I checked my message. "Janice says they are waiting outside a testing center that Mel just went in." I raised my eyebrow. "Shall we investigate?"

Marcus flashed me a crooked grin. "Nah, they've got it. Besides, I know a really nice place to take you to make up for my bad driving."

I laughed. "Okay, this place better have a five-star rating."

Marcus smiled and I relaxed into my seat. We did our part of the investigation, so I'd leave it to Nate and Janice to do the rest today.

Chapter Eleven

Marcus

We found Janice and Nate in a corner booth at the Sheetz gas station on the outskirts of town.

"Hey guys," Janice said, as we approached the table. "How was your date?"

"Delicious," Alissa said. "The restaurant has an amazing pasta primavera."

"Well, while you all are discussing food," Nate said, "I'd like to talk business."

"I'm not done yet," Alissa said. "I need to know why you're drinking a slushie in this cold weather."

Nate took a sip. "Can't a man enjoy the finer things in life?"

"Good one, Nate," I said sarcastically. "How about we discuss why Mel was at the testing center for two hours."

"And how does she know Mr. Maddox?" Alissa asked.

"Sounds juicy," Janice said. "Who's Mr. Maddox?"

Alissa and I filled them in on what we found — Mel's apparent nervousness, Genesee Country Club, the white Cadillac, and Mr. Maddox. Nate looked on as Janice scribbled down everything into what looked like a flow chart. She drew a line that connected Maddox to Mel.

"We need to find out the connection between Mel and Maddox," Janice said. She marked the line with a hurried question mark. "Let's find out tomorrow."

"There's something else," Alissa said. She bit her lip as she looked to me. "This has been bothering me, Marcus. What does your father have to gain if we discover what's really going on?"

"When we discover what's really going on," Nate correct. He eyed me as he took a long slurp of his slushie. "But Alissa's right. We've been wondering the same thing."

I gritted my teeth and made eye contact with each of my friends. Janice and Nate exchanged a knowing glance.

"I hate to say this," said Nate. He sighed. "I think we need to add Mr. Kahale to our list of suspects."

"He's not a suspect," I said defensively.

"Right, sorry," Nate said. "I meant to say client. Still, someone needs to find out what your father has to gain or lose when we uncover the mystery surrounding this alleged enrollment scandal."

"I'll do it. Maybe I can look around my dad's home office."

"Okay, so onto the next matter of business," said Janice as she stood. "Lis and I will handle Mel and Abby tomorrow."

"Definitely," Alissa agreed as she stood. "We'll be seeing them both for the sports meeting."

"And we'll be seeing Derrick and whoever else is on our list tomorrow now that we've joined the basketball team," I said. I looked to Nate. "Right, bro?"

"I'm not looking forward to basketball, so please don't remind me," Nate said. He loudly slurped his slushie.

Seeing Nate's bad mood made Janice and Alissa laugh. We all knew Nate preferred to work with gadgets and stay up to date on the latest spy techniques. He rarely did any after-school activities, so the basketball team would be a huge commitment.

Now that we had our assignments, we were ready to get back to work. Everyone seemed pumped, but I was panicked. I needed to find out what Dad had to do with all this tonight.

That night, I sat up in bed and listened to the quiet of my house. Occasionally, my phone would buzz. Another message notification from Instagram. I hadn't looked at any of them, but I figured now would be a good time to start.

Scrolling through my feed, I realized someone had tagged me in the video at Abby's party. Going to my messages, I saw mixed comments: some sprinkled with envy that they didn't think of it themselves and others demanded an apology. For what? If only I knew what happened, then I could say something. I wanted to respond in the comments, but I left the matter alone. Then, I came across a direct message from Alissa telling me to check out her profile.

I knew she couldn't resist Instagram, I thought.

I went to Alissa's profile and found a few pictures of us together. After hitting like on all of them, I set down my phone and listened.

In my parent's bedroom, Dad snored. Mom claimed she found it soothing, but I thought differently. Normally, I put in my earbuds and listened to music to block the snores until I fell asleep. Though I didn't take Dad to be the amateur-sleuth type, I imagined he must've been collecting data on Lenape High's graduation and college enrollment rate. Otherwise, he wouldn't have recruited us to get close to find out what some of our classmates knew. It would've been helpful if Dad clued us in on what we were looking for. But I didn't think he'd tell me if I took the direct approach. On our ride back to the house, Alissa said she'd be on call if I needed anything. This explained why she suddenly had time for reactivating her account.

Well past midnight, I got up. Taking my tactical pen from my nightstand should I need a flashlight, I crept toward my bedroom door. Popping it open just a crack, I listened to the gentle rhythm of sleep from my parents' bedroom. Opening the door more, I took a glance at Bri's door. Darkness filled the crack between the bottom of her doorframe and the floor. I stepped into the hallway and crept down the flight of stairs. Once in the middle of the living room, I froze. There was movement upstairs. When all was silent again, I let the paranoia of being followed set in. Positioning my flashlight to the stairwell, I turned it on. If anyone had been there, I didn't hear a retreat. I brushed off paranoia and concluded the house had settled a bit. Breathing easier, I made my way to the basement steps. Dad had a home office down there all to himself. If he'd been collecting dirt on anything or anyone, he'd have it locked up securely. One creeping step at a time, I kept my hand on the railing and descended the steps. Once downstairs, I turned the flashlight back on, letting its bluish glow illuminate the darkness before me.

Our finished basement, sparsely furnished, housed an obstacle course of unused gym equipment. I eased my way around some free weights, an elliptical machine, and a bench press. Once outside of Dad's office, I took a deep breath and reached for the door. When I grabbed the knob and turned, it didn't budge. Jiggling the knob again resulted in the same.

"I knew you were up to something," said a familiar voice.

I turned and shined the flashlight in Bri's face. She blinked several times while keeping her hands planted firmly on her hips.

"Stop shining that light in my face," Bri demanded.

"I will once you tell me what you're doing here," I whispered.

"I could ask you the same. You're lucky you didn't wake Mom and Dad up."

I sucked my teeth. "Just go back to bed."

"Tell me what you're doing, or I'll scream."

Experience told me she would, so I caved. "Fine. Dad recruited Alissa, Nate, Janice, and me to get close to some kids at school. He thinks they are cheating the system. I need to find out how."

Bri sat and crinkled her nose. "Is that all? I thought you were doing something more exciting. Well, here take this." She tossed me a lock-pick kit Nate had given to me.

I caught it. "Seems you've been watching us closely."

Bri crossed her arms. "Yup, now get on with it, so I can see what you're looking for."

Handing the flashlight to Bri, I took out the tools I needed and knelt by the door. After a few minutes, it popped open. Once inside Dad's office, Bri shut the door behind us.

"Where should I look first?" she asked as she swiveled the flashlight around the office.

"Try that file cabinet over there," I said. "Let's see if it opens."

Sure enough, the cabinet door opened. I began to rummage through the drawers. Finding nothing but bills, birth certificates, tax papers, and real estate information, I closed the drawer.

"What're you looking for?" Bri asked.

"Maybe student records, or something," I said.

As Bri shined the light across the desktop, it illuminated a flash drive plugged into the computer's USB port.

"Dad was working on something," Bri said. She

touched the mouse, causing the computer to whir to life until it came to a log-in screen.

"Guess Dad locked the computer," I commented.

I was ready to guess Dad's password, which I doubted consisted of any combination of names or birth dates for Bri or me. I pulled the chair forward until my feet bumped something. Glancing under the desk, I noticed an unmarked filing box. I stood, picked up the box, and put it on the chair.

"What're you doing?" Bri asked. "I bet I could guess Dad's password."

"Hold on a sec," I said. Opening the box revealed several tabbed filling folders, each labeled with initials — M.A., W.M., A. J., D. K. — and others I didn't have time to examine before Bri grabbed the one labeled W.M.

"I wonder what they mean," she said as she opened one of the folders.

I took out the one labeled M.A. When I opened it, I recognized what looked like student records, or names redacted. Still, I realized this must've been the evidence Dad had been collecting. While I skimmed the folder, Bri gasped beside me.

"I really don't think we should be looking at this stuff," she said.

"Why?" I asked.

Bri handed me the folder she'd been looking at. It was my turn to gasp as I stared at our school financial records. Then it clicked. The initials W.M. could only stand for one person. While taking that person down could result in a promotion for Dad, I doubted he'd be motivated by power and position. I knew my dad valued honesty. He didn't like fraud and he didn't like it when people cheated the system.

Now, I understood why he recruited us. If we played it right, no one would suspect us of working undercover to get close to our classmates. He had bits and pieces of information, but not enough to bring it to the police. He needed something clearly incriminating.

"We should go," I said.

Bri nodded. After putting everything back and closing the door behind us, we crept up the basement stairs. Once in the living room, the light flicked on. On the sofa sat Dad in his robe. He glared at Bri and me.

"Bri," he said, "go to bed, and no lingering on the steps."

"But I didn't do anything," Bri whined.

"No buts, young lady."

Bri clamped her mouth shut. She walked by Dad and me and stomped up the stairs. Her door slammed. A minute passed before we heard a creaky noise from upstairs.

"Bri, I know you're listening," said Dad. "Please go to bed."

"Oh brother," Bri huffed. She shut her door again.

"Now, onto the matter at hand," Dad said. "Did you find what you were looking for?"

"I found a box," I admitted sheepishly.

"And what did you find in the box?"

"Financial records, but I didn't get a good look. Also, I found...some academic records."

Dad nodded. "You saw enough. Marcus, you and your friends need to know one thing. Someone is cheating the system. I need you and your friends to find out how, okay?"

"But what does that have to do with our classmates."

Dad grinned. "That's for you and your friends to find out. Anything I need to know?"

I thought for a moment but decided not to tell him about Maddox and Mel. "Nope, nothing to report. Um...good night, Dad."

Dad narrowed his eyes. "Good night, son. But you tell me when that nothing becomes something, okay?"

Chapter Twelve

Alissa

As usual, the four of us met at lunch the next day. With nothing new and my sorry attempts at catching up with Mel throughout the day, we had nothing. I spotted Mel and Abby sitting across from each at their usual spot. Abby picked at her food while Mel appeared to message someone.

"Janice, you don't happen to have that blouse with you?" I asked.

"Yeah," said Janice, "let me go get it."

"What are you about to do?" Marcus asked.

"Just watch," I said as I stood.

Nate chuckled. "I think we're about to be schooled."

"You betcha!" I exclaimed. I left Marcus to roll his eyes as he and Nate watched me leave.

Leaving my tray with Marcus and Nate, I

walked on over to the table where Mel and Abby sat. Both seemed engrossed in their phones. They didn't even look up when I approached them. I wasn't exactly sure what I was going to say, but my gut instinct told me to talk with Mel and Abby. Taking a deep breath, I plopped myself beside Mel.

"Hey, girl," I said cheerfully.

Mel flipped her phone face down on the table and looked at me. Her face turned a shade of red.

"Oh, hey," Mel said. "What's up, Lis?"

"Oh, you know," I said. I smiled and swiped a lock of hair behind my ear. "I figured I'd check in with you two about joining the lacrosse team. Is there any word yet?"

Abby snickered. She put down her phone, too.

"What a random question," Abby said. "You came all the way over here just to ask us that? I'm sure coach will let us know who made the cut soon enough."

"Well, it's not just that," I said. I looked to Mel. "Do you think we could talk for a sec?"

"Oh," Abby said mockingly. "Are you cutting me out so soon?"

As if on cue, Janice scooted in next to Abby.

"Here, you go," said Janice. "I wanted to return this." She handed Abby the blouse she had borrowed on Saturday. "Thanks again."

"Seriously, I said you can keep it," said Abby as she slid the blouse over to Janice.

Janice's face fell. "Oh, yeah right. I totally forgot. Still, my mom said I should return your blouse. She wanted to know where you got it, so I can keep up with the trends." Janice scoffed. "Tell me. Do I look trendy to you?"

Abby looked her up and down. "It looks like you've already got the trends figured out, but I can fill you in."

As Abby and Janice chatted, I leaned into Mel.

"Is everything okay?" I asked. "I tried to catch up with you yesterday after school, but it looked like you were with someone."

"So, you saw that?" Mel asked. "I guess I'm not that surprised. I was talking to my uncle. It was a family emergency. Don't worry about it."

She glanced at Abby and Janice. As she talked about make-up, Janice bobbed her head and caught her attention. I couldn't let my conversation with Mel end like this. I needed more information.

"I understand, Mel," I said. "We're good." I cleared my throat. "By the way, I was thinking about getting a part-time job. Do you know—"

"I thought you wanted to play lacrosse," Mel said as she cut me off.

"I do," I said. "I'm thinking of doing more of a weekend gig."

Mel opened her mouth to speak, but her phone started to flash. I tried to peek at the caller ID, but Mel grabbed her phone before I could see the number. She stood.

"I've got to take this," Mel said. She walked away.

"Looks like that's my cue," Abby said. She got up to leave and Janice nudged her.

"We should go shopping sometime," Janice said.

Abby sighed. "Sure, fine. Whatever, Janice.

Listen, I've got to catch up with Mel. I'll see you tonight."

"So, Abby, does that mean I'll see you later, too?" I asked.

Abby looked to me and flashed a half-smile. Then, she turned and walked away. Janice scooted closer to me and winced.

"I can't tell if Abby vibes with you," she said.

"Me neither," I replied.

Janice shrugged. "You and Mel seemed to be having a nice conversation. Did she tell you anything?"

I sucked my teeth. "Not sure. Mel seems to be hiding something. What about Abby?"

"I think we should get to know Abby. She seems super nice once you connect with her. Honestly, I have no idea why she would want to go to Penamore College. She, like, knows everything about cosmetology."

I nodded as I watched Abby and Mel leave the cafeteria. "Mel seemed to be in a hurry when she got a phone call just now. Do you think we should go follow them?"

Janice grinned. "If we're gonna do that, we should probably do it now."

"Okay, one sec." I shot Marcus a text to have him and Nate pick up our things from our lunch table. Somehow, I knew they'd understand.

"You read?" Janice asked.

"Yeah, let's go," I said.

We exited the cafeteria just as a thin stream of our classmates did the same. Soon, the hallways filled up. Although I'm sure I was being rude, I pushed through the hallways because I needed to find Mel. Janice trailed behind me. Since Mel's little encounter with her supposed uncle Mr. Maddox in the parking lot, she'd become the target of our investigation. A good thing, too, especially since she was going in the wrong direction. Our next class, A. P. Statistics was on the north end of the building. We were headed east where half the school seemed to converge at an intersection that led to the athletic wing of the building. At the intersection, Mel disappeared into the fray.

A gap revealed Mel and Abby heading down the athletic hallway where Mr. Kahale's office used to be. Stepping through the gap, Janice and I followed Mel and Abby down the hallway. When they reached the exit door, Janice and I ducked behind a trophy case. At the end of the hallway, the door popped open.

"They've exited the building," Janice whispered as she peeked around the trophy case.

"Well, let's see where they went," I said.

As the bell rang, we scurried toward the exit. Once at the door, I slowly opened it. Looking through the door and seeing no one, we took a few cautious steps. When we stepped outside, Janice turned and caught the door before it closed. She pulled out a pencil, which she used to prop the door open a crack in case we needed to get back inside.

A cold gust of wind passed over the parking lot, causing us to shiver. We pulled our thin hoodies over our heads.

"Why is it so cold?" Janice asked.

"I don't know, but if you keep talking, they may

hear us," I whispered.

"Wait, look over there."

Across the parking lot, Mel and Abby didn't even bother to look behind as they appeared to head toward Mel's car. Before they got to their car, Mr. Maddox's Lexus sedan pulled up beside them.

I nudged Janice. "That's the car Marcus and I followed yesterday."

Mel and Abby ran toward the car. Without looking back, Abby opened the front passenger door and got in. Mel, on the other hand, seemed a little more hesitant. As she glanced around, she seemed to look in our direction. Fortunately, we were too far away, so they didn't seem to recognize us. A moment later Mel got in the backseat. Nothing about Mel's behavior suggested this Maddox guy was her uncle.

"I don't like this," I said. I ran to my car, and Janice followed me. She caught my arm.

"Lis, what are we doing?" I asked.

"We can't leave them like this," I said. "We need to go after them to make sure they're okay."

Chapter Thirteen

Alissa

"Turn right!" Janice shouted.

"I know," I said. I kept the Lexus at least a block ahead of me. "Besides, I've been here before."

I followed the Lexus through the same familiar, narrow streets Marcus and I had passed yesterday. Then, the driver ahead of us took a sudden sharp right.

"GPS says we've passed the country club," Janice said as she continued to track the directions on her phone.

A block ahead, the Lexus took a sharp left. When I came to the corner, it was nowhere in sight.

"Where'd they go?" I asked.

"They couldn't have gone far." Janice peered out the window as we passed several side streets.

Bringing my car to a slow roll, I glanced out my window to try to pinpoint the Lexus. In my console, my phone buzzed. Janice picked it up and unlocked it with the password I gave her.

"You got a text from Marcus," she said. "He wants to know where you...uh-oh." Janice paused. "Your mom is calling."

"Ignore that," I said. "Hmm...tell Marcus we've passed the country club."

Janice typed a response. "The school office must've called home. We're all gonna be in trouble."

I shook my head. Mr. Kahale most likely wouldn't cover for us. I tried not to think about what my parents would say when I got home. I inhaled and exhaled. Focusing on the mission was more important.

"There it is!" Janice shouted. She pointed to the right. I spotted the Lexus in a parking lot of what appeared to be an unmarked brick building. I rolled past it.

"I'm going to park around the corner," I said.

After parking, we kept ourselves close to the walls of a warehouse. Careful to avoid tripping over sidewalk cracked from general lack of maintenance, we made our way toward the brick building. From the outside, just like the surrounding industrialized area, the building seemed abandoned. Though only a few blocks away, Genesee Country Club stood pristine amidst a sprinkle of boutique shops and some well-known chain restaurants.

We came to the unmarked building and its dilapidated parking. Beyond the rusty chain-link fence, the Lexus seemed out of place.

"I see a door over there," Janice whispered. "Do you think it's unlocked?"

"There's only one way to find out," I said.

Keeping to the side of the building, we crept toward the door. The door appeared pale and green with rust. I gripped the handle and pulled. The door creaked open. Janice and I cringed. Hopefully, no one would be alerted to our entrance.

"Wait," Janice said. "Let's turn off our phones." She pulled out her phone and turned it off. I nodded and did the same.

We inched our way down a set of steps lined by walls of solid oak on which lamps were intermittently mounted. Once at the bottom of the steps, Janice motioned for me to take the lead. We found ourselves in a dimly lit hallway, one much longer than the outside of the building would have suggested.

Somewhere ahead of us we heard muffled voices growing louder as we continued down the hallway until we stopped at a door. The voices came from the other side. Leaning closer to the door, I listened.

"Is that what you pulled me from class for?" Mel asked.

"I'm not complaining," Abby said.

"Listen, you two," said a vaguely familiar female voice. "Something has to change with your acceptance."

Janice and I exchanged a look. The woman's voice seemed vaguely familiar, but through the door, I couldn't recognize her. I leaned in closer to hear the conversation.

"But it's not that simple," a man, whose voice I didn't recognize, said. "We don't want to involve your parents. They've got a lot on their plates as they plan for the gala."

"That means we need to come to agreement," added the woman. "Don't you think so, girls?"

"What kind of agreement?" Mel asked. "I legit earned this."

"You did," the woman replied. "But we can see to it that it can be unearned as well."

I imagined Mel staring, mouth agape, at what these people had said. None of it made sense to me. I wondered what it all meant and desperately wanted to stay to hear more. A tug at my sleeve pulled me out of the moment.

Janice pointed down the other end of the hallway. Footsteps were approaching. Our exit was blocked. We needed to find another way out of here and fast. Ripping myself away from the door, I followed Janice down the hallway. As we turned the corner and waited, I heard the previous door creak open.

Although I wanted to know who came through the door, I stayed focused on the direction we were headed. Janice took a quick peek around the corner. In the same instant, she turned back toward me.

"Let's keep going this way," Janice whispered.

"I wish I knew where we were going," I replied flatly.

I followed behind Janice while the footsteps behind us seemed to cease. The walls of this hallway, like the others, were made of solid oak and lined with electric lamps that let off a warm, yellow glow. A cool breeze went across my face. Any other time I would've welcomed it, but the breeze smelled musty.

"Do you smell that?" I asked.

"Smell what?" Janice asked. "Oh, wait." She stopped at a door that was slightly ajar. "Obviously I don't know where this goes, but we might as well check it while we're here."

"This is possibly the worst idea, ever," I said as I followed Janice through the door.

She turned on her flashlight. "Or maybe it's the best idea and we just don't know it yet." The light on her tactical pen illuminated the beginnings of a tunnel. Beyond the light, the surroundings appeared pitch black.

"Where do you think this goes?" asked Janice

"No idea," I said. "We should head—"

"I think they went this way," echoed voices in the hallway behind us.

Without hesitation Janice ducked into the tunnel. Once she entered, I came in and closed the entry behind us. I turned and pulled out my tactical pen, ready to use both the light and the far more defensive end.

As we jogged down the tunnel, our lights bounced off walls stained with rust and water marks. Both the tunnel's unfamiliarity and oppressive darkness made our run feel much longer than it really was. After what I imagined to be a few hundred yards of straight up nothing, we came to another door. Janice reached for it and tried the lever.

"It's locked," she huffed.

"Can you pick the lock?" I asked. "I think they're gaining on us." I heard the sound of footsteps from behind us.

"I think I found our way out," Janice said. She grabbed a skeleton key resting on a hook to the left of the door. She shoved the key into the lock.

As the key jiggled, I heard the distinct sound of metal, creaking on hinges and coming from the other end of the tunnel. I shut off my flashlight, leaving Janice and I in the dark. Janice cursed.

"I can't see," she whispered.

"Do the best you can," I whispered.

Footsteps and muffled voices echoed off the tunnel walls. If I could hear them, I assumed they could hear us. Down the hallway, circles of lights reflected on the tunnel walls. Whoever was following us was coming closer. Once again, Janice jiggled the key. The lock clicked.

"Here goes nothing," she said.

Janice opened the door wider and we both slipped through it.

In one seamless motion, I pulled the door shut and grabbed the key from Janice. Stuffing the key into the lock, I turned it, clicking it into place. Gripping the handle and pushing down on its release lever and pulling for good measure, I was satisfied the door was locked. I sighed as I turned toward Janice.

"Let's hope they don't have a key," I said.

When I looked forward, I was in awe of the space. The rest of the room featured a decorative luxury. The room was furnished with a pair of red velvety sofas and four matching wing-back chairs. Mounted on the oak walls were antique lamps. On one wall was a placard that read Genesee Country Club, Our Legacy and Our Future.

Janice stood with her back to me as she snapped some photos of the placard.

"We don't have time for that!" I yelled.

"I'm capturing clues," Janice said. She glanced at me and pointed at some names written below the placard's title. "A couple of the names on the placard look familiar, so I was taking some pictures."

"That's not a bad idea. Just be quick about it."

Janice smirked. "So, you admitted it? This is the best idea ever had."

I chuckled. "Fine. It's the best idea."

The door leading back through the tunnel jiggled.

"Time to go," Janice said. "Let's try this way!" She pulled open the door, leading to what I hoped to be our escape.

In my pocket my phone buzzed several times, telling me we'd gotten several text messages while we were underground. In the hallway, I glanced to my left and observed a trash can on wheels being pushed out of the room. To my right, Janice was already reaching the exit door.

"What are you kids doing in here?" an older man asked.

Janice shoved the door open, which triggered an alarm. Bells rang around us as she and I ran toward my car, not even making an attempt at stealth.

Chapter Fourteen

Marcus

"Have you heard from the girls?" I asked Nate. We headed out the building at the end of the day, bags strapped over our shoulders. Nate checked his phone.

"No, I haven't heard from them since the text they sent us a couple of hours ago," Nate said.

Around the side of the building, I spotted Derrick, Trae, and a couple of other guys on the outdoor basketball court. "Maybe we should cancel our little pick-up game with these guys and go look for them."

Nate waved nonchalantly. "They can handle themselves. If they need us, Janice would text."

Feigning confidence, I added. "You're right. We've seen what they can do." While that last part was true — Alissa could take down a grown man

— I wasn't so sure about Nate being right.

Nate jogged on ahead and went through the entryway of the steel mesh gate that closed in the court. Not quite as enthusiastic as Nate, I passed through several steps behind him. While Nate set his bag on the fence, Derrick dribbled and passed the ball between his legs.

"Hey, guys!" Derrick called out. "Are you ready to play?"

"Do you think those fancy moves are gonna help you today?" I asked jokingly.

Derrick laughed while Trae joined him. "Actually, I caught up with Trae and he wanted to tell you two something." Derrick nudged Trae, who cleared his throat.

Nate came over. Though it was cold, he wore shorts.

"What's happening now?" he asked.

"I'm sorry about the other day," Trae said. "I was just messing around. Let's call a truce." He offered a hand.

With some hesitation, Nate took it. "Don't worry about it, bro. I haven't thought about it since then."

Although I appreciated Trae's apology, I wasn't sure how sincere it was. I thought back to Justin's warning and wondered if Derrick was somehow setting Nate and I up for something.

"Now that's over, shall we play?" I asked.

"Yeah," Derrick said. "Drop your things off and join us on the court."

I jogged over to the bench, but Alissa still remained on my mind. If she was in trouble, she'd let us know. I was sure of that. Just as sure that she and Janice wouldn't put themselves in a situation where they would be without their phones. I sent her a text and waited for a response. I stared at my screen for a minute.

"Hey, Marcus!" yelled Derrick. "Are you joining us or are you just going to stand there?"

"Hold on a sec!" I called.

An Instagram notification from Alissa popped up: *Can't wait to see you again. Let's meet at our usual spot.*

Seeing her message made me smile. I wondered why she decided to send me a direct message instead of a text, but I was glad to hear from her anyway. I set the phone down and joined the others on the court.

"Nice of you to join us," Derrick said. He checked me the ball.

"Sorry," I said as I easily caught the ball and looked at the others. "I was just a little distracted."

"Relax, bro," Nate said. "The girls are good."

"Yeah, relax," Derrick added.

"Okay, let's go," I said. I forcefully checked the ball back to Derrick.

Though not quite enough for a full court, we split up in two teams.

"Marcus, you play point guard on your team," said Derrick. "Nate, you play forward."

The others on our team seemed to already know what they were playing and needed no further instruction from Derrick. I concluded he was most likely the team captain of the varsity team.

Throughout the game, our teams remained

even. During one play, Nate passed the ball down center toward me. I caught it with ease. As I turned to shoot, someone, shouting in the distance, pulled me out of the moment. In that moment, someone from the opposing team knocked me to the ground. As I searched for the source of the shouting, Trae and I locked eyes for a second. He offered me a hand.

"I'm sorry," he said. "I thought you—"

"No worries," I replied as I cut him off. I took his hand, and he pulled me to my feet.

After the commotion stopped, I looked around until my attention landed on Ms. Calhoun and Principal Moss frantically chasing papers around the rear parking lot.

Even though we were in the middle of a game, I jogged off the basketball court and crossed the parking lot to help Ms. Calhoun and Principal Moss. I didn't want them to lose their stuff, so I snatched up a few papers. From what I could tell, the papers looked like filled in bubble sheets.

"Looks like you dropped these," I said as I handed Ms. Calhoun the stack I'd gathered.

"These are private," Ms. Calhoun snapped. She snatched the papers out of my hand as she stood. "You have no business with them."

"Here's some more," Nate said as he stepped between us.

Looking around, I noticed Derrick, Trae, and the others had come to help. They handed the rest of the papers to Moss. The principal approached Ms. Calhoun and me.

"Is that all of it, Ms. Calhoun?" asked Moss.

"I think so," she replied. She fumbled through

the papers and nodded. "Gentlemen...thanks for your help."

"It's not every day we have students as conscientious as you," added Moss. He paused and looked to each of us, but his gaze seemed to linger on me. "I trust none of you took the liberty to peek at any of these...tests."

"If you did see them, don't worry," Ms. Calhoun said. "Just don't share what you saw with your peers."

"Right," Nate said. He scratched his chin. "But out of curiosity, was there a test I missed?"

"No," said Ms. Calhoun as she stepped forward. "These are for A.P. students."

"Let's get these to their proper location," said Moss. He directed his attention to us. "Again, gentlemen, we thank you for your help."

Ms. Calhoun fidgeted with her stack of papers. "Thanks. Take care of yourselves."

Leaving Calhoun and Moss, Nate and I headed toward the basketball court with the others to practice layups. When we passed through the gated entryway, Nate stole a quick glance.

"Why are Moss and Calhoun just standing there?" he asked.

"No clue," I said. I picked up my phone. "What do you think those tests were?"

"Hey!" Derrick shouted from the court. "Are you guys done talking?"

"Not yet," Nate said. "Got a few questions for you, though."

Derrick dribbled the ball as he came over. "What's up?"

"You're in a couple of A.P. classes, right? Did

you take a series of tests?"

Derrick shrugged. "We haven't had any tests recently and we don't have any coming up either."

"That's weird," I said. A notification from Alissa showed on my phone and heat rose to my face. Derrick and Nate looked at me, even though I tried to avoid eye contact.

"Is your girl texting you?" Derrick asked.

"Yeah," I said simply. "It looks like I'll have to cut this short. We'll see you tonight." I looked to Nate. "Can you give me a ride?"

Chapter Fifteen

Marcus

Nate pulled his Jeep up to a curb and stopped near Slices on the Avenue.

"I'm telling you, bro," said Nate. "Those messages sent to you through Instagram don't sound like Alissa."

"Whatever," I said. "We meet up here all the time."

"Sure," Nate said. "But we've got about an hour before that sports meeting tonight, and the girls are coming from downtown." He took out his phone. "Let's get their ETA."

I sighed. "I'm really starting to doubt myself."

Nate typed out a text. "Janice hasn't mentioned anything about Alissa's account. And you know how she is with that."

I stared out the window at the red and yellow

bold lettering for Slices. A couple walked into the restaurant. Inside, I could see movement — guests catching an earlier dinner.

"Woah!" Nate exclaimed. "Look at this message I just got from Janice." He handed me his phone, and I read the message.

We're kinda in the middle of something. Why would we want pizza right now?

I passed him back his phone and gripped mine.

"If that wasn't Alissa contacting me, then who was it?" I asked.

Nate shut the Jeep off. "Only one way to find out."

Nate and I got out of the Jeep, letting the doors close with a satisfying thud. I sent Alissa, or whoever I was texting, a message that I would be late tonight, even though Nate and I were about to head inside now. We scanned the area — sedans and SUVs parked headfirst in spaces and shoppers, checking out windowed goods before they stepped inside to warm up. If there was anything unusual, I wondered if he and I would even notice.

"Go ahead," Nate said. Nate motioned for me to cross the street. "Whoever you're meeting shouldn't see us together."

"How do you know this person hasn't seen us already?" I asked. I knew I was cramping Nate's style, but I had to ask.

Nate frowned. "You're right. But I still think you should go in alone. You know, just in case."

When I came to the door of Slices, I looked down one end of the avenue. When I looked down the other end, Nate sat on a bench and scrolled through his phone. Somehow, he managed to cross without me noticing. I watched as various patrons entered the restaurant. Everyone else I could see seemed to go about business as usual. I confidently grabbed the door handle and pulled, which caused the bell on the door to chime welcomingly.

There were several seating options, including a counter and a booth. I sat at a booth and made sure I faced the door. From where I sat, I could also see outside. A group of girls about my age approached. One of them glanced in the window, which made my heart race. I wondered if this was the poser, pretending to be Alissa on Instagram. The girl at the window took out make-up, applied some, and then moved on. I watched her as she left, then I chuckled.

Suddenly, I was aware of a presence beside me. A strawberry scent wafted in the air. I turned to see a girl smiling at me.

"She's cute, isn't she?" asked the girl.

"I'm sorry," I said in a daze. I was momentarily mesmerized by her light brown eyes. "Who are you?"

She laughed. "Don't play like you don't know me. We were supposed to meet right now."

I laughed nervously. "Oh, right."

She slapped me playfully on my shoulder. "You are too much. We've been chatting on Instagram today and last night. See!"

She held up her phone, displaying a stream of messages apparently between us. I went to reach for her phone to get a better look, but she moved it. The girl slid beside me in the booth, blocking me in.

"Like I said," she continued. "We're connected."

"Okay." I stood up. "I don't know what's going on, but I didn't send you those messages. I've got to go."

The girl pouted and tugged my sleeve. I wasn't sure how I would get out of this situation, but then I saw Nate coming to my rescue.

"There you are," he said. "Sorry, I was running late, Marcus. Who's your friend?"

The girl stood as she glanced from Nate to me.

"Who's he?" she asked.

"This is my friend, Nate Wilson," I said.

Her face flushed as she gawked at me. "I thought it would just be me and you. This was a mistake." She got up, shoved me, and stormed out the restaurant.

"Do you know who that was?" Nate asked.

"No," I said. "I forgot to get her name." I glanced out the window and made eye contact with the girl before she disappeared. "She claims she knows me. Apparently, she's the one I've been talking to on Instagram all day."

"I told you it wasn't Alissa," Nate said. He headed for the door. "Let's try to catch her."

I had to take several long strides to keep up. We spotted the girl just as she disappeared around the end of the building. At the end of the block, Nate and I peeked around the corner while catching our breath. I spotted the girl as she opened the side passenger door to the Cadillac sedan that had followed Alissa and me yesterday. With the door fully open, she glanced our way, and I could've sworn she shook her head. She ducked into the car and slammed the door shut. Thereafter, the Cadillac rolled off while Nate and I pressed ourselves against the side of the building. As the sedan passed, the tinted windows made it impossible to see the driver.

"Crap," I said. "We were so close."

"Do you think she's with the Genesee Country Club?" asked Nate.

Before I could answer, my phone and Nate's phone started to buzz. I pulled out mine and saw a text from Alissa. I started to read it.

Um... babe. Pretty sure there's a logical explanation for this. Can't wait to hear it.

The second text included a picture of me, sitting with the girl that met me at Slices.

"Nate, do you see this?" I asked in shock. "Who took a picture of me with this girl?"

Nate looked at the picture and cringed.

"Sorry," he said. "I played lookout, but somehow missed her lookout."

"Guess we can't catch everything," I said. "Let's go."

Once in the Jeep, I thought about what I'd tell Alissa. I'm sure she had some explaining to do, too.

Chapter Sixteen

Alissa

We can see to it that it can be unearned.

I recalled what the mystery woman who spoke with Abby and Mel, had said. Sitting in the parking lot, Janice and I examined the photos she managed to capture from the country club. I had suspected Abby to be involved, so I wasn't surprised to find her last name Jenkins listed on the placard. Albright, Mel's last name, would've been a surprise if I hadn't followed her and Abby to the country club.

I surveyed the parking lot and hoped to see Mr. Maddox in his Lexus or a Cadillac driving off. If either vehicle had been in the parking lot, we missed it. I suspected Abby and Mel were dropped off before Janice and I arrived.

"How does all of this connect?" I asked aloud.

"Leave it to us to figure that out, right?" asked Janice. She winked.

I picked up my phone. "What's taking Marcus so long? I'm trying to figure out who sent me this photo of him with that girl."

"Maybe you should call the number, but block your caller ID."

"I did that already. The number went to an automated response, saying the number wasn't in service." I sighed. "Hey, this is sort of bugging me, but do you think Marcus is cheating on me?"

Janice held my hand. "Oh, Lis. Marcus is so into you he literally doesn't look at any other girls. Don't worry about it."

I smiled. "Thanks, girl. I guess the only thing we can do now is head to the gym."

As we got out of the car, Janice yelped.

"Oh, no!" she squealed. I forgot to put the key back!" She held up the skeleton key.

"Good thing it's too old to be tracked," I said. "Drop the key in the center console in my car. We'll figure it out later."

Once Janice secured the key, we walked toward the gymnasium entrance. Mel ran in our direction with Abby, trailing behind her.

"I'm so happy you all decided to sign up!" she yelled.

"I'm not," Abby said flatly. "You all can't be serious." She crossed her arms.

"What's the problem?" asked Janice as she stepped forward. "Are you scared I'll take your spot?"

Abby laughed. "You nearly took my head off last semester in P.E. with a volleyball. Do you really think you can handle lacrosse?"

Janice squirmed, but she didn't back down. "Actually, I thought I could learn from the best. Maybe you could teach me a few of your moves." She smiled sincerely.

Abby narrowed her eyes. "You two just watch it."

"Well," Mel said politely, "I hope you both make the team."

"Mel, would you stop being so nice?" Abby asked. "Let's go. This meeting's about to start." Abby whisked Mel away before she could say anything else.

At first, I wasn't sure, but now I believed Abby looked down on us. Given what we discovered at the Genesee, I guess she had her reasons.

"Abby is starting to get on my nerves," said Janice.

"I think she feels the same way about us," I replied.

I directed my attention at the door as Coach Dunbar and Mr. Kahale, our admin on duty, entered to greet parents and students. As we followed them in, I glanced at the parking lot one more time to see if any suspicious cars were out there. Still nothing.

"If you're worried about the boys, don't be," Janice said. "It's not like there's serious danger lurking around the corner."

"You're right," I said. "It's probably nothing."

Janice nudged me. "I'm know I'm right. You should listen to me more often."

We both laughed as we took our seats in the gymnasium.

Coach Dunbar took the podium, beginning his

speech on the importance of commitment. A few minutes later, Nate took a seat by Janice. They started to whisper, so I directed my attention to the back of the room. Marcus stood to the side engrossed in his phone.

He better not be talking to that girl, I thought.

When Marcus looked up, he stuffed his phone in his pocket and took the seat next to me.

"Crazy day, right?" he asked.

"You got that right," I said. "We've got some plans to make. Something's going down at—"

"The country club," Marcus interjected. "I know."

From the podium, Coach Dunbar seemed to raise his voice, bringing his spiel to a close. "All right, gang," he said. "This'll be a great season. You'll find coaches at their respective tables, with sign-up sheets for spring sports. I'll be here if anyone has any further questions."

Parents and students shuffled out of their seats. The four of us remained seated and scooted in closer to each other to exchange notes.

"So, we followed Abby and Mel to this old building connected by a tunnel to the country club," I said. "Somehow we've got to get back there. There's this placard with some names we need to look into."

"There's also the shady sounding convo we overheard," Janice added. "Somehow they're into something that has to do with grades and acceptance."

"We sort of already knew that," Marcus said. "But now we have a location."

"Seems like we, I mean, you have a lot more than that," Nate said. He lightly jabbed Marcus. "Why don't you tell them about the girl you met?"

Marcus pulled his collar and looked to me. "Alissa, I don't know who that girl was. I didn't even get her name! She swears I've been talking to her through Instagram. But I haven't. I was talking to you."

"Nope," I replied. "I haven't used my account in years. I was going to reactivate it, but I got interrupted."

"See, Marcus," said Nate, "I told you that girl you that wasn't Alissa sending you DMs."

"Well," said Marcus. His ears turned red. "That's...um." He paused.

"I think the word you're looking for is embarrassing." I tapped my foot as I waited for him to continue.

Marcus scratched at his neck. "I'm sorry, babe. I was confused. I think she was using your account and I still don't know why she wanted to meet up with me."

"Meet up with who?" asked Mr. Kahale as he walked up to us. He grinned. "I didn't catch it all. But if it's about Marcus, then I agree." Then he directed his attention on Janice and me. "As for you two, we have camera footage of you following Abigail Jenkins and Melanie Albright off the premises. You skipped half the day today. That means three hours of after-school detention."

"Sorry," Janice and I said simultaneously.

"How about this?" asked Mr. Kahale. "You tell me what you found out."

"Yes, sir," I said.

"Good. I will talk to you four later." Mr. Kahale smiled and walked away.

As Janice and I parted with the boys, I spotted Abby, Mel, and a few other girls I recognized from P.E. class. Mel glanced my way, but quickly averted eye contact when Abby looked my way.

Janice tapped my shoulder. "Let's go sign up before the spots are full."

Joined by our parents, we went over permission slips and student athlete contracts. I scanned the room for Marcus. He and Nate stood in the basketball line and talked with Derrick. Marcus was joined by his mom. Nate's parents were nowhere to be seen. Knowing his home situation, I imagined something truly did come up that kept his parents from coming to the school. His mom worked full-time, and his dad didn't keep a job for long.

As Mrs. Kahale took the papers from the basketball coach, Marcus pulled out his phone again. Knowing him, I imagined he wanted to get to the bottom of the messages sent from my account. To be honest, so did I. Someone spoofed my account, and we needed to find out why. I only hoped Marcus would wait for me this time, so we could work as a team. I'd definitely need them around if I ever came across that girl again.

Someone waved a paper in my face.

"Alissa Imani Claude, do you hear me talking to you?" asked my mother.

"Sorry, Mom," I said. "I was distracted."

She furrowed her eyebrows. "I can see that. What's bothering you, honey?"

I took the paper, signed it, and gave it back to my mother. "It's nothing."

She narrowed her eyes. "I know that look. Okay, whenever you're ready to talk, I'm here."

I saw Janice and her mother finishing up with their paperwork. "Thanks, Mom. I'll catch ya back at home."

"Don't stay too long." She turned and headed toward the front door.

A moment later, Janice joined me.

"Good news!" Janice squealed. "I'm going to hang with you guys tonight, so we can plan out our next move."

"That is good news," I said. I looked around for Marcus, but I didn't see him. "Did the boys leave already?"

Janice pursed her lips as she scanned the room. "Maybe they're outside waiting on us."

"Must be following another lead," I said, spotting Mel looking intently at me. "Hold on a sec."

Leaving Janice behind, I approached Mel and waved. She looked beyond me, then turned away. I stole a look over my shoulder. There was no one there.

I sighed. A part of me suspected Mel knew we followed, though I didn't know how.

Janice ran up to me. "Lis, we have a situation. We have to go."

Seventeen

Marcus

I stood there staring up at a boy about my age, only much wider and taller than me. To my right stood Nate, staving off the guy's sidekicks. To my left, Derrick did the same. The boy shifted his weight on the balls of his feet and cracked his knuckles.

"Man, I know you've been with my girl, so stop playing dumb," said the boy.

"I already told you," I said. "I don't know what you're talking about."

Apparently, he didn't like that answer. The boy swung at me, but I managed to sidestep his blow. Although he stumbled, he quickly recovered. He came at me again, but Nate placed himself between us while pulling something out of his pocket. In the same movement, Nate blocked the boy's outstretched arm and jammed the object quickly into the inner arm of the bicep. The boy cursed and grabbed at his arm. Commotion to my right and left drew my attention as the boy backed down.

Our classmates and some parents had gathered around us as police lights flashed. Accompanied by an officer, Dad pushed through the crowd.

"That's enough, boys!" Dad yelled.

"Everyone back away," the officer commanded.

The crowd of kids and parents dispersed. Another officer approached and signaled to us.

"You three come with me," said the other officer.

"Marcus," said Dad. "I'll join you shortly. I'm going to work on crowd control first and then talk to your friends Janice and Alissa about what they found."

Alissa caught my gaze in the distance. I nodded as I trusted her to give Dad just enough information. Though Dad could be trusted, we still suspected him of hiding something from us, maybe for our own protection. I watched as Dad caught up with Janice and Alissa and led them into a building.

I caught up with Nate, Derrick and Trae, all of whom were already at the police squad car with a tall, athletic man.

"I can assure you, officer," said the man. "I'm Trae's dad, and these boys had nothing to do with any of this." He made a sweeping gesture of the parking lot to include Nate and me in his generalization.

"A few statements, starting from the beginning,

are all we need right now," said the officer. He directed his attention to me. "Marcus Kahale, right? Why don't you go first since you were the apparent target of this attack? Have you and this boy met before today?"

"He doesn't even go to our school," I said. "I don't even know his name. The four of us were in the parking lot talking about open positions on the basketball team when this guy and his two friends rolled up on us."

"We just finished with an athletic meeting for spring sports," Derrick added.

"Is this meeting an exclusive event?" asked the officer. "Outsiders aren't permitted?"

"None," Trae piped up. "But we sometimes—"

"Watch it son," Trae's dad said sternly.

Trae ignored his father and continued. "Anyway, we sometimes see these guys coming over here to use our outdoor court. But we've never had any real interaction with them." He finished with a glance over at the other boys, who were on their phones, while the officer with them had his arms crossed and scowled.

"We don't know their names, or what their issue is with Marcus," said Derrick.

"All I know is," Trae said, "no one messes with Marcus or Nate."

"Did you have anything to add, young man?" asked the officer.

I looked to Nate, who rubbed his neck.

"I don't have any other information to add that they haven't said already," said Nate. "Can we go now?"

The officer folded his pad, tucking it away in his

front pocket and looked at me. He handed me his card, then handed one to Nate, Trae, and Derrick. "Hold tight. Let me check with my partner."

When the officer was out of earshot, I turned to Derrick and Trae.

"Thanks for covering for me," I said.

Derrick held up his hand.

"Don't mention it, bro," he said. "Now that you're on the team, Trae and I have your back."

"Thanks, I guess," said Nate.

Even though I welcomed new allies, I felt like our friendship with Derrick and Trae seemed too easy. I wondered if Nate thought the same thing as me. There had to be a catch to having friends like Derrick and Trae.

Derrick pointed in the direction of the other squad car. "Don't look now, but here comes company."

The two officers escorted the other boy over.

The second officer spoke first. "Sounds like a misunderstanding between Tyler and Marcus. He doesn't want to press charges."

"Who's pressing charges?" asked Dad.

We turned to see my dad, glaring at both officers. "From what I heard after interviewing several witnesses, including parents, this boy here should be the one worried about charges against him. Not to mention, he doesn't belong on school grounds. Mr. Long here was kicked out five years ago, which puts him at least at twenty years old."

The officer escorting Tyler looked at him. "Son, I'm going to need to see that ID again. He directed his attention back on us.

"Gentlemen, if you'd excuse us."

With wide eyes, Tyler Long protested as the officer escorted him away.

Something about this entire situation felt off, but I didn't know why. As the others looked on, Trae's dad spoke up.

"Well, boys, it's been a long night," he said. "Trae, let's get going."

"Okay, dad, just let me say one more thing to my friends," said Trae. He turned to us. "Nate, about your books...I was just messing around. I didn't mean anything by it when I put your stuff in the trash at P.E. class."

As Trae's dad looked between his son and Nate, he rubbed his chin. I could tell this was the first time he had heard of this instance between Nate and Trae. As Trae turned to leave with his dad, Derrick waved to us.

"See you around," he said.

When the others left, my dad looked at Nate and me. He had a concerned expression. The temperature seemed to drop the longer we stayed outside, which made me feel cold. I wasn't sure what he was about to say, but I didn't think I would like it. I braced myself.

"I'll get right to it," Dad said. "The girls told me about everything you've been up to. I'm sorry I brought you all into this mess."

"But, Dad," I said, "we're so close to figuring things out."

"And you've done a lot. I think it's best I take it from here. There's another thing. Principal Moss will be talking to the girls tomorrow. I think you know about what. Don't be surprised if he wants to talk to you two about the fight you just had.”

“I guess that makes sense,” Nate said. “But that other kid started it.”

“I’ll have all that in my reports,” Dad said. “With any luck, that’ll be enough,” Dad said. “Listen, I’ve got to lock up. Marcus and Nate, you two sit tight. I’ll be driving Marcus home tonight.”

As Dad walked off, Alissa and Janice joined us. I noticed Alissa shivered, so I wrapped my arms around her. She smiled faintly.

“Looks like this case is grounded,” Alissa said.

“But your dad doesn’t know everything, Marcus,” Janice said. “For one thing, we didn’t tell him we broke into the country club.”

“I’m impressed,” Nate said. “What did you find?”

While Janice chatted about the tunnel and the list of names on a placard inside one of the rooms, I looked on as the officers cuffed Tyler Long and helped him into the patrol vehicle.

“Does anyone else feel like my encounter with this Tyler Long wasn’t a coincidence?” I asked.

My friends all gave me a conspiratorial look.

“Too bad we don’t know who his girl is,” Alissa said mischievously as she gave me a quick kiss.

“Yeah, I sure wish we weren’t off the case,” I said jokingly. “I don’t know what I’m going to do now.”

“Whatever you say, boss,” Nate said. He chuckled.

“Whatever you have planned, Marcus,” said Janice, “I’m in.”

We all snickered, but quickly grew quiet once

Dad returned.

"I don't know what's so funny, but you all need to go straight home," he said. "The detective work is over."

"Yes, sir," we said in unison.

"Good," Dad said. "Your parents, even yours, Nate, will be waiting up for you."

"Okay," Nate said. He turned to Janice. "Did you want to ride with me?"

"Yeah," Janice said. "Just let me get my hugs in."

Janice hugged Alissa and waved to me while Nate gave me a fist bump. They headed into the Jeep. Meanwhile, I walked Alissa to her car. She wrapped her arm in mine.

"Don't get me wrong," Alissa said. "Your dad's cool, but this case isn't over. We've still got work to do."

"Most definitely," I replied. "Let's just lay low for a while and work with our evidence."

Alissa sighed. We reached her car, and she entered the driver's side. She closed the door and keyed the ignition to let the car warm up.

"I'm sure Moss'll have something to say about Janice and me cutting school," she said.

"But you won't be alone," I said. "Moss has to talk to Mel and Abby because they skipped school, too. At least, you and Janice had a good cause."

Alissa laughed. "That's true. You sure know how to cheer me up, Marc." She winked. "I'll see ya tomorrow."

I waved as she drove off. Though we only lived next door to each other, there was a finality to the whole thing. I hadn't ridden home with Dad for a month. I returned to Dad's station wagon where he was already waiting for me in the car. After climbing in and letting the door slam shut, I waited. I sensed he had more to say.

"Son," he said. "I mean it. You and the others will need to lay off this case...permanently. I don't want to have to say it again."

"Yes, sir," I said. I knew that if my dad said something more than once, he meant it. As we drove off, I noticed Dad's jaw clench. I had seen this look. Something had happened, and I knew Alissa and the others would be there to help me figure it out.

Chapter Eighteen

Marcus

Slowly, I walked down the hallway to the guidance counselors' office. I hoped I wasn't in trouble. Before my name was called on the intercom, I had been engaged with my group mates Trae, Rayna, and Krista in a good discussion about symbolism found in The Fall of the House of Usher. Though I wouldn't consider any of them my friends, I did like our group discussions. They were better than our usual classes where Mr. Cifra talked at us and only one or two kids participated.

I guess I could say I wasn't too surprised that my group hadn't harbored any ill-feelings toward the Instagram video from this past weekend's little fiasco at Abby's house. Most gossip in high school had a lifespan lasting of less than a week.

When I got to the door leading into the counseling office, someone called me from down the hallway. I glanced over to see Nate.

"What are you doing here?" he asked.

"Ms. Calhoun wanted to see me about something," I said.

"Same with me. What do you think she wants?"

"I'm sure it's nothing."

As we stepped into the counseling office, the secretary looked up.

"Ms. Calhoun will be with you shortly," she said.

"Thanks," Nate said. He reached for a candy dish on the secretary's desk. "Do you mind?"

She smiled sweetly. "That's what they're there for."

Nate and I pocketed a few pieces of candy. While we stocked up, Ms. Calhoun came down the hallway from her office.

"Right this way, gentlemen," she said. "This shouldn't take long."

"Oh, good," I said as we walked down the hallway back to her office. "We were in the middle of a really cool conversation in English class."

Nate gave me a you-must-be joking look and I shrugged. When we reached Ms. Calhoun's office, she gestured for us to sit. Nate and I plopped in our chairs, while Ms. Calhoun remained standing. She looked between Nate to me, but mainly focused on Nate's loud candy crunching.

"I'll get to it, then," she said. She pulled a manila folder from her shelf and sat down as she opened it. "I had three hundred and thirty-seven papers in my pile, but some of them of have gone missing."

I pulled out my own piece of candy, letting the wrapper crinkle.

"Did you want us to help you find the missing tests?" I asked.

"Yeah, we're pretty good at finding things," Nate added.

Ms. Calhoun remained quiet. She watched as I opened my candy and Nate ate another piece.

"I was hoping that maybe you picked up a handful of papers and forgot to give them to me," she said.

"Why would we do that?" I asked.

"Yeah," said Nate with a mouth full of candy. "Besides, it's not like we were the only ones out there. Derrick and Trae helped us get the papers, too."

"That's enough," Ms. Calhoun said forcefully. She cleared her throat. "I mean, that will be all, gentlemen. Thank you for your help. You may leave now."

"Yes, ma'am," Nate and I said in unison. Sensing our cue to leave, we rose from our seats.

"Wait!" Ms. Calhoun exclaimed as she handed us each a pass. "I just wanted to say one more thing, and I don't mean anything by it. If someone were to find those papers in their possession and returned them to me, let's say, anonymously, that would be great!" She nodded and forced a smile that didn't reach her eyes.

"We'll be sure to spread the word," I said. "Have a good afternoon, Ms. Calhoun."

Leaving Ms. Calhoun to fume, Nate and I exited her office. When we were around the corner and halfway down the hallway, leading to Mr. Cifra's classroom, we burst into laughter.

"What was her deal?" Nate asked.

I laughed. "She was probably annoyed by your candy-eating."

Nate shrugged. "Really? I thought I was being soothing."

I shook my head. "Nah. I'm pretty sure she thinks she really took those tests."

Nate combed a hand through his hair. "Honestly... if I had time, I would've looked through them."

"Really?" I asked.

"Only if it'll help with the case." Deadpan, he gazed at me, then broke into a grin. "I'm kidding... maybe."

I shook my head. "Let's just head back. I'm glad we got out of there when we did."

We resumed our walk to my classroom. Janice rounded the corner in front of us, with her head bowed.

"Good to see you, too!" Nate cheered.

She stopped and glowered at us.

"I'm really not in the mood," she said.

As Nate took a step back, so did I. Janice normally seemed energetic, and I wasn't used to this touchy side of her.

"I'm sorry for whatever I did," Nate said. "I won't do it again."

"That's a lie," said Janice. She laughed drily. "It's not you. It's me. I'm headed to the principal's office and I'm not looking forward to it."

"Isn't Alissa going with you?"

"I wish. I think Moss'll talk to her later. Sorry,

guys, I gotta run before Moss wonders where I'm at. Toodles!" She sped away.

"We should hurry back," I said. "I'll catch ya at lunch."

"Yeah," Nate said. He headed in the opposite direction of his class. "I'm gonna walk a bit."

I went straight to class. To my disappointment, however, the groups had already been rearranged into rows. Since my classmates were busy reading, I went straight to Mr. Cifra and handed him my note from Ms. Calhoun. In exchange, he handed me a slip of paper with a writing prompt on it.

"You should be fine," Mr. Cifra said. "Your group says you really know your stuff."

I relaxed as I returned to my seat and opened my binder. Inside my binder I found a stack of papers, the missing test papers. I balked at the sight of them.

How did these get here? I thought.

I looked across the room at my group members. I glanced around the room. Rayna's face was practically on top of the paper as she wrote vigorously. Krista sat upright with her legs crossed and her back to me. Trae seemed to just hover over his paper, writing nothing. None of them seemed the type to have stuffed missing tests inside of my binder. Their sudden appearance also seemed too coincidental to be coincidental.

"Marcus," said Mr. Cifra from his desk, "this work is due today."

I nodded and glanced quickly at the essay question. My topic would be how one small crack in the wall of a house in ill-repair represented the fracturing of an ancient family. That, I realized is what we needed to find. That one small crack that would split this case wide open and end a legacy that we could only loosely connect to this case. We needed to find out how some of our classmates were getting into these prestigious schools with such poor grades. We needed to put pressure on those people identified from Dad's list. Between the four of us, I knew we could recall every name.

Chapter Nineteen

Alissa

I shifted to the edge of my seat as Principal Moss swiveled the computer monitor toward me. My parents, sitting on either side of me, gave me a quick glance before returning their attention back to Principal Moss.

"Now, Mr. and Mrs. Claude, I was as surprised as you were when I found out Alissa cut class yesterday," Moss said. He placed his glasses on his desk and stole a glance at me as he continued to speak. "So, what I'm going to show you here is truly telling."

"Go ahead," my father said. "Let's see it."

As Moss directed his mouse over the play button, I let out a slow breath as if willing the tension to leave my body. He clicked play.

The video opened with a wide angle shot of

Janice and me leaving the cafeteria. My mother couldn't resist letting out a disapproving grunt as the video cut to Janice and me turning down the hallway leading to the athletic department. As I watched, I imagined music playing and building in suspense as another angle showed us by the exit. On the recording, we glanced around before exiting the building four minutes after noon. With a smug look on his face, Moss clicked the video off and directed his attention toward me.

"Now, what've you got to say for yourself, Ms. Claude?" Moss asked.

I sank in the seat. I couldn't believe what I'd seen. Janice and I had followed Mel and Abby, yet that video made it look like she and I left for no reason. I maintained eye contact with Moss for a moment as I tried to breathe evenly. I had a feeling that no matter what I said I couldn't get out of this situation. I sat up straight.

"We just wanted to cut class," I said. "That's all."

"There's gotta be more to that!" exclaimed my mother. She turned to my father. "Richard, you know no daughter of ours would ever just cut class."

"Alissa, what's gotten into you?" he asked. He frowned.

I shrank lower in my seat. Choosing silence over saying anything incriminating seemed to be my best option. Still, I couldn't help but wonder if pursuing this case was worth it. I felt like my friends and I were taking all the risks while Mr. Kahale sat back and told us what to do.

"Very well, then," Moss said. He put on his

glasses. "You do three consecutive days of after-school detention." He stood and shook hands with my mother and father. "Thank you both for coming in. I'm sure your daughter has learned her lesson." He turned toward me. "Right, Ms. Claude?"

"Yes, sir," I said flatly. "Am I free to go?"

"Yes. Take this with you," he said.

He handed me a pass. When I grabbed it, Moss seemed to hold the pass tight, forcing me to catch a reflection of myself in the lenses of his glasses as he searched my eyes. When he released the pass, a chill tingled down my spine.

"Thank you, sir," I said, turning away.

My mother scrutinized Moss for a moment. "Is there something else you needed, Mr. Moss?"

"That'll be all," Principal Moss said. "You folks take care."

I walked with my parents to the main office. My mother shook her head.

"Something's not right about that man Mr. Moss," she said. "I don't like him."

"Me neither," I said. "Three days of detention is way too harsh."

"You're still not off the hook," my father said. "If you skip class again, we won't let you hang with your friends after school."

"Just be good, okay, sweetie?" asked my mother. "I see the Kanes over there, so your father and I are going to say hello before we go."

My parents signed out of the office and greeted Janice's parents in the vestibule. Though I couldn't hear them, I imagined my mother giving a fair warning to them about Moss.

As I turned toward the office door, leading out to the rest of the school, I spotted Janice coming toward me. Her head appeared to be down, but her face brightened up when she saw me. "Hey, Lis!" she squealed. "You're already here."

"Yeah, my parents and I just finished up our little talk with Moss," I said. I leaned in closer to her. "By the way, he's going to show you an altered video. Let's talk about it during lunch."

"Thanks for letting me know." Janice sighed. "Okay, time to face the music."

I watched as she and her parents went inside. Then, I marched to class. This afternoon, before detention, we'd meet up at lunch. Somehow, I knew the four of us could recall all the names on the list Mr. Kahale had handed us. Then, Janice and I would be able to make good use of detention this afternoon by checking those names against the ones from the placard at the Genesee Country Club.

"Ladies and gentlemen," Ms. Berry said that afternoon as Janice and I, along with several others, arrived for after-school detention. "Please place your cellphones in the caddie at the front of the room." There were several groans, but a steely-eyed glance from Ms. Berry stopped all that.

Janice and I waited in a short line of high school stereotypes, ranging from jocks to recluses, as they turned off their cellphones and secured them by Ms. Berry's desk.

"Oh, I almost forgot," Janice said. She slipped me the photograph she'd taken of the placard at the country club yesterday.

"Nice," I said. I grinned. "When did you have time to print this?"

Ms. Berry shushed me. I could hear the warning in her voice. My peers stared at me as if I should've known there should be absolutely no talking. I apologized as I stuffed the photographs inside my notebook. Ahead of me, Janice shut her phone off. Then it was my turn. When I turned around, I saw that most of the other students had taken seats several desks away from others, so I did the same.

Ms. Berry walked to the center front of the room and stood where she kept a close eye on us for the next hour.

"Most of the faces I recognize as my regular crew," she said. "Some of you are new." She seemed to intentionally avoid looking at Janice and me.

Janice raised her hand. "Ms. Berry, will anyone else be joining us?"

"Why would you ask that?" Ms. Berry asked. Someone in the back of the room sniggered but stopped when Ms. Berry glared in the back.

A shade of pink colored Janice's cheeks. "I was just wondering. That's all."

"This is everyone." She gave a thin smile. "Now, I want to remind you there will be no talking and you need to remain seated."

Janice's mouth dropped, but she stayed quiet. I wanted to scream. I knew what Janice was thinking. Mel and Abby should have been here. When this was over and we headed to practice, I intended to find out how they managed to avoid detention. I opened my notebook and began to work through scenarios. Some scenarios were as innocent as no one noticed Mel and Abby at the scene. Other scenarios I concocted were more underhanded where they must have worked out an arrangement with the administration that allowed them a pass. I looked at the list of scenarios and began to scribble out everything that sounded like a crazy conspiracy theory. A tap on my shoulder distracted me from my work. Ms. Berry stood over me.

"Alissa, you're a star athlete and an honor student," she said. "I'd hate to see that go down the drain for something as silly as cutting class."

Is she threatening me? I thought.

I stared at her. She backed away and continued to survey the classroom. I made eye contact with Janice, who gave me this weird look. I wasn't sure what to make of Ms. Berry.

Looking back over my notes, I flipped the page and added Ms. Berry to my list of suspects involved in this apparent plot to fudge your way into a prestigious school.

Glancing at the clock, I sighed. There was still another half hour to go before this detention would be over.

Chapter Twenty

Marcus

Players were getting in their pre-practice warm-ups when Coach Mason came in and blew his whistle. He was followed by Mr. Cifra.

"Let's hit the bleachers," Mason said.

When we were all settled, he introduced Mr. Cifra as the new assistant coach and Derrick as our team captain. Both stepped aside, giving Derrick the floor.

"Most of you know each other already," he said as he grinned and glanced at the team. "But let's introduce the newbies." He motioned for Nate and me, along with a few others, to stand.

As we did so, the rest of the team applauded. When the cheering died down, we sat. Derrick continued to introduce the rest of the team. As I tracked each introduction, making mental notes about whether these new guys would play forward, center, or guard, I noted that Justin, who sat a little off to the side, avoided eye contact. Oddly, he wasn't wearing a uniform.

After finishing the last introduction, Derrick stepped back to let Coach Mason continue.

"If you haven't noticed, there's twenty-one of you on the team," he said. That means some of you will start and play every game, while some of you will be rotated out. But don't worry. You're all a big part of the team. I don't intend to cut anyone, but I will if you're not giving it everything you've got in practice. All right, let's break you off into scrimmage teams."

Once finished, we hit the courts where we drilled some plays for a half hour.

At break, I spotted Justin sitting on the benches and writing vigorously in a notebook. This time he wore metal framed glasses that occasionally slipped off his nose as he wrote. With a water bottle in hand, I approached him.

"Hey, Justin," I said. "I'm surprised to see you out here."

"I could say the same about you," he replied. He adjusted his glasses.

I tilted my head. "What's that supposed to mean? I tried out for the team and I made it."

Justin lowered his voice. "Listen, I'm a team manager. I belong here. I don't know what strings Derrick pulled to get you on this team or why. Just be careful."

The whistle blew. Coach Mason called us to the courts.

"Blue and Green, you guys take right court," he

said. "You others, take left. I'll referee the right side while Coach Cifra referees the left. Play hard and play your best. Today will help us determine starting positions."

"Hey, coach, can I talk to some of the newbs for a second?" asked Derrick. "I just wanted to give Marcus and Nate some pointers." Coach Mason nodded. Derrick signaled for us to follow him.

We went to the corner of the gymnasium where we huddled into a circle. I caught a glimpse of Justin watching us from the bleachers, much too far away to overhear anything.

Derrick lowered his voice. "I need you to do me a favor. You know, quid pro quo, and all that."

"Are we in your debt, or will we be in yours?" Nate asked.

Derrick waved off the comment. "Doesn't matter. What's important is we help each other, as a team, you know? Besides, everyone knows you're like detectives."

"Okay," I said nervously. "Tell us what you need us to do."

"Here it goes," said Derrick. He stepped closer and lowered his voice. "I need you to find out what Abby's up to. She's ghosting me, man. I think she may be cheating on me."

I choked back a laugh. "That's not our—"

"We got you, bro," Nate said as he cut me off.

"I knew I could count on you guys," Derrick said. "Now let's get out there and show our coaches what you've got."

We hit the courts. Not long after, we were subbed in. Somehow, I thought Derrick may have had something to do with that. With no time to mull that over, I caught a ball. I was in play and that's all I needed to focus on at the moment.

At the end of practice, Nate and I found Justin, earbuds in and waiting on the curb. Approaching him from either side, we ensured he wouldn't be able to take off.

"Did you need a lift?" Nate asked.

"No, I'm good," said Justin as he removed an earbud. "My parents will be here soon."

"Tell me what you meant by be careful," I blurted out.

Justin removed the other earbud. "Derrick likes to ask for favors. When I told him that I needed another extracurricular activity besides coding club for my college application, he said he'd do me a favor by getting me on the basketball team. Derrick spoke to Coach Mason, and then the position for team manager opened."

"So, what did Derrick ask for in return?" Nate asked.

Nate and I studied Justin's face. He cringed and fidgeted with his earbuds until he decided to stuff them in his pocket.

"It was a long time until I received my instructions by text from a Google number. I was told to edit some cloud footage to make it look like you guys crashed Abby's party. When I was done, I uploaded the video to a folder. That video is the same one you saw on Instagram. I had no more business with it after that."

"Whoa!" Nate shouted. He held up a hand. "So, Derrick does know something about the video? Wait, how'd you know it was a favor?"

A car pulled up. The passenger side window

rolled down. Justin's mom waved and he headed for the car.

"See you guys later," Justin said. He climbed into the car and closed the door with a resounding slam. As the car pulled away from the curb, Justin gazed at us with a stern expression.

"Are you thinking what I'm thinking?" I asked Nate.

"Yeah," he said. "That dude Justin acts way too old."

I shook my head. "No, that's not it. I think Justin is doing someone else's bidding. That's the favor."

"Oh..." Nate paused. "And maybe that favor is for the person that owns that Instagram account laxislife362."

I nodded. "Now, you're getting it. There's one other thing, too." I fished out Calhoun's missing tests and handed them to Nate.

"So, I know we're supposed to be off the case and all, but this is way too big not to share." He grinned. "Let's meet the girls."

We got in Nate's Jeep and exited the parking lot. While Nate drove, I texted Alissa to meet us at Slices.

On the way to the restaurant, I couldn't stop my leg from shaking. I wondered if Derrick's "proposed assignment" was somehow a ruse. Plus, its timing coincided too easily with my finding of those papers, especially since Derrick was right next to us as we helped Ms. Calhoun gather up the stray tests. Whatever it was, we'd approach with caution.

Chapter Twenty-One

Alissa

"Look who finally showed up to practice!" Abby called out from the field when Janice and I arrived.

Ignoring her comment, Janice and I placed our bags on the bleachers. After detention, we'd changed into our lacrosse gear. We just needed to put on our cleats. As we did, I noticed the formations. Spread out on the field in smaller groups, the girls practiced running, dodging, and shooting. One of our coaches spotted us as we tied up our cleats. When she came over, she frowned.

"The sports program doesn't look too favorably on players who make a habit of landing themselves into after-school detention."

"I'd like to say it won't happen again, but we've

got two more days of this," said Janice as she stood.

"But it's all for the same incident," I added quickly as I finished lacing up.

"So, I heard," said the coach. "Another incident of skipping school, and you're out." Coach turned toward the field and pointed. "Alissa, you join Mel's group. Janice, you join that group over there."

While we jogged with our lacrosse sticks in hand to our groups, Janice gave me a knowing look.

"Make sure you get Mel to talk," she said.

"I'm on it," I replied. We parted ways and I stepped into Mel's group of four.

"Hey, everyone," I said. "Coach said to join you."

"Sure thing," Mel said. "You all know, Alissa, right?"

I received a mixed welcome. Two girls smiled and waved. The last girl twirled her lacrosse stick and stared.

"Tough break about getting detention for skipping," she said.

Mel stiffened at the remark. She managed to force a smile.

"Anyway, Lis," Mel said. "We're gonna practice some quick stick drills." While the others lined up facing us, Mel explained. "This'll focus on communication and fast releases. We won't be cradling or using the non-dominate hand for this one. Stand at the end facing me, just like others, okay?"

Like the other three, I held up my stick. Mel

passed the ball to the first girl, who passed it quickly back to her. The same drill repeated for each girl, so I felt like I could get it. When it was my turn, Mel seemed to launch the ball at me much harder than she did the other three. When it landed in my net, I dropped the stick.

"C'mon, Lis," Mel said. "You've got to grip the stick a little tighter than that."

The girl who'd twirled her stick earlier sniggered at this comment.

Without remark, I picked up my stick and tossed the ball back to her — stick high. Mel caught and released the ball to the first girl, second, and then the third until it came back to me. Though the ball landed in my net with a thwonk, I kept my grip on the stick.

"Good job," Mel said. "Let's do this a couple more times before the next drill."

When we switched to another drill, Mel directed me to the center while she and the others stood at either corner to receive and pass the ball to me. This time I knew for sure her passes to me were much harder and much faster than the other girls. A few times I had to shift stances to receive the ball, or risk getting smacked in the face or chest. By the time coach blew the whistle for break, I needed to address Mel's microaggressions.

"Hey, Mel, I couldn't help but notice the way you passed the ball to me."

"What about it?" she asked.

I blinked twice as I was taken aback by her response. "Are you mad at me?"

She took a swig of water. "Nope. Let's get to the

field. It's time for a little scrimmage."

Mel set her water bottle down and ran off. Following her, I noticed Janice out of the corner of my eye. She and Abby were running together, passing a ball between each other until we'd all regrouped in center field.

Once we were all gathered, Coach split us up into four separate teams that would each play on opposite sides of the field. Mel directed me to take up attack position by her side.

Back and forth we played the shorter field. Sometimes, I missed or fumbled the ball. Other times I scored or assisted. For my first game, I could've done worse.

At the end of practice, Janice and I returned to our benches while the rest of the girls packed up their things.

"How'd it go?" I asked Janice as we set our lacrosse sticks down.

"I should've done this a long time ago," Janice said. She shot me a thumbs up.

"It also looks like you and Abby are friends now."

Janice laughed. "I got her to warm up to me. She actually wants to hang out sometime. Can you believe that?"

I struggled with a knot. "I wonder what came over her."

Janice pulled off her cleats. "I guess time will tell."

As I got my own knot loose, a pair of cleats came into view. I looked up to see Mel standing there.

"Can I sit?" she asked.

"It depends," I said. "If you still have that passive-aggressive energy going on, we can talk later."

Mel shook her head. "I'm sorry about earlier. I didn't mean it."

"Okay, you can sit." I scooted over.

She sat. "Lis, you're my friend. Whatever you think you're doing; you need to back off."

I raised my eyebrow. "Are you talking about lacrosse or something else?"

"I think you know the answer to that." She leaned into me. "It isn't safe for you...or me."

I searched Mel's eyes. "Is you're life in danger?"

She sighed. "I guess safe isn't quite the right word. I have to go." She smiled weakly at both Janice and me before she left.

When Mel left, Janice and I packed our things away quickly and headed to my car. On our way, I received a text from Marcus.

This is definitely not over. Meet us at Slices.

"Did you tell them we've got something to share?" I asked.

"I sure did," said Janice as she popped the rear passenger door open.

I laughed as we tossed our things in the back seat of the car. Once buckled, I pulled out of the parking lot. As Janice flipped through the radio stations, I mentally flipped through my encounters at lacrosse practice today.

"What do you make of Mel's warning to back off?" I asked.

"Of course, there's nothing on the radio," she said. "Anyhoo, I think she and Abby are involved with the Genesee. That's why they didn't have to do detention."

"I wonder why it was so important for those people to meet with them during the day. It's not like it's a super-secret place."

"That tunnel we found was super secretive, though." Janice squealed. "Hold on! I love this song!" She turned up the music.

As I drove along, Janice sang to a song about a small-town girl and a city boy. At the chorus, I joined in. We sang like that until we came to Slices. Once parked, I turned the car off, thus bringing our little fun to a close.

The door chimed as we entered the pizza shop. At our favorite booth, Marcus and Nate were sat cozied up in in sweatpants and sweatshirt. With drinks in hand, they talked animatedly.

Janice and I exchanged a look and sashayed on over to the table.

"Guess you boys have been busy," Janice said. She slid into the seat beside Nate.

I did the same next to Marcus. "But I bet our news is bigger than yours," I said as I sat beside Marcus.

I didn't wait for either them to blurt out their little news. I filled them in on everything – the no-shows for detention Abby and Mel, the warning from Mel to back off, and Janice's friend invite from Abby.

"This is nuts!" Marcus exclaimed.

"Yeah, that's big news," Nate said, "but we have a little side case."

"And what might that be?" I asked.

Nate smirked. "Derrick wants us to keep an eye on Abby because he thinks she's cheating on him, and we found out that kid Justin created that video from cloud storage. He doesn't know whose account posted the video, but we think it has something to do with laxislife362."

"And that's not all," Marcus said. He pulled out some papers from his backpack. "These are the missing tests Ms. Calhoun was asking us about earlier today. She called us into her office because she thought Nate and I took them. When I came back to class, I found the tests in my binder."

"Let me see those," I said. I took the papers, thumbed through them, and handed them to Janice.

"Wait!" Janice exclaimed. "I know these names! Lis, where's your notepad?"

Chapter Twenty-Two

Marcus

An hour and a whole pizza later, a list of the names of our classmates and a notebook filled with ideas sat in front of Janice.

She flipped through the notebook as Nate huddled closer to her while he slurped his soda. Janice pushed him away.

"Cut it out, Nate," she said. "I'm trying to concentrate here." She didn't even take her eyes off her notebook. "I'm trying to find something we missed."

"We need to get back inside The Genesee," Alissa said. "Why don't you and Nate be our lookout while Janice and I go undercover?"

"I'm sorry," Nate said. "I'm pretty sure I've seen that scenario play out a thousand times on NCIS, and it doesn't work out. Besides, Mr. Kahale said not to do anything illegal."

"Too late for that," I said.

Janice shushed us.

"Look at this, you guys," she said. "It's a sketch."

She turned her notebook toward us. Nate shook the ice in his cup before he downed a few scoops.

"Is that a floor plan?" he asked as he crunched on the ice.

"No, silly, it's a map that shows the tunnel through the Genesee," said Janice. She dragged her finger over the map from the building through the tunnel. "How old do you think that tunnel is?"

"If I were to guess, I'd say it's two hundred years old," said Alissa.

"Yeah, but those buildings in the area by the Genesee can't be older than thirty or forty years," I said.

"Doesn't matter," Nate said. "Say we use those tunnels to get the Genesee. Then what? What are we looking for?"

Janice's confidence waned as she spoke. "There was the room Mel and Abby were in. Why'd those people take them there? Maybe that's where they keep records of whatever dirt they might have on people like Mel."

Alissa chimed in. "They did say her acceptance could be rescinded if need be."

"But why?" I asked. "That we can tell, she has no association with the country club, except through Abby."

"Speaking of whom," Nate said. "We still have to tail her. See what Derrick thinks she's up to."

"I'll do one better," Janice said, picking up her phone and sending a text. "I'm gonna see if she wants to go shopping Saturday."

Alissa's face brightened with a smile. "I'm down with that. See if Mel wants to come along."

"When did you two become friends with Abby Jenkins?" I asked.

"At lacrosse practice," Janice said without looking up from her phone.

While Janice texted, Nate rested his elbows on the table. "Let's say she's game. We've got to check out the access tunnel."

I nodded. "Our safest bet is the library. There's probably some kind of public archives we can look at."

"Ah, man!" Nate seemed to whine. "But I have some night vision goggles I've been wanting to try out."

Janice raised an eyebrow. "I don't want to know." In the next breath she turned her attention on us. "Abby says, how about tomorrow?"

"I can swing that," Alissa said. "What about Mel?"

Janice confirmed with a nod. "Tomorrow. Right after practice."

I shot a glance at Nate. "Too easy, right?"

"Maybe," Nate said. He wrapped an arm around Janice. "But my girl can make friends with anyone."

Janice pushed him away with a laugh. "Please!"

"Listen," Alissa said. "We should probably head back before our parents start blowing up our phones. C'mon, Marc. I'll drive you home."

As she and I stood, Nate held up a hand. "Just a sec. If anyone asks, we were in a study group."

I surveyed the room. "Pretty sure we weren't being watched. But okay."

"Nate," Janice said. "I'm pretty sure they're not taking you seriously. Still, I'm dying to know about these nights vision goggles you have."

Alissa rolled her eyes. "See you two later."

As Alissa and I headed out the door, Nate began to talk excitedly about his new toy while Janice interjected with an occasional uh-huh. If I was a betting man, I'd say she was feigning interest for his sake.

When we turned down our street, a black sedan pulled away from the house.

"That looks like the same car that belonged to the man that was talking to my dad after Abby's party," I said. "I haven't seen it around since then."

"Me neither," Alissa said as she pulled into her driveway. "I don't think we've met the owner."

I pondered. "Not unless he's Maddox or the guy who owns the Cadillac."

Alissa snorted. "We can rule both of those guys out, I'm sure."

After grabbing our things and wishing each other a good night, I entered the house. My grin disappeared at the sight of my parents waiting for me in the living room.

"Where've you been," Mom said. "I thought you were supposed to be home right after basketball practice?"

"He was," Dad said. "You should've been

waiting for me right outside, son. Are you intentionally disobeying us?"

From where I stood, I heard the top of the stairs creak. I didn't have to look to know Bri hovered on the landing just out of sight. I sat down by Dad.

"Something's come up."

"Something?" Mom asked. "Marcus, you're going to have to do better than that."

I kept my attention focused on Dad. "Something I need to talk to you about."

"I'm sure whatever you have to say to your father, you can say in front of me," Mom said.

Dad stood. "I'm afraid it's not that simple, dear. Please excuse us. I'll fill you in later."

Mom remained tight-lipped and left the room. Dad turned toward the basement door. "C'mon. Let's chat downstairs."

As I followed Dad into the basement, Bri's thumping footsteps announced her entrance onto the main floor. I bet she wanted to know what my punishment would be. Once in the basement, Dad and I maneuvered around workout equipment and other rarely used odds and ends until we came to his office door. I noted he replaced the lock with a keypad.

"I added this security feature to keep the critters out," Dad said.

I nodded, even though I knew dad was trying to keep more than just critters out of the basement. He turned his back toward me, so the door was covered. The keypad beeped four or five times in rapid succession. The bolt clicked and Dad opened the door.

Once in the office, I noted some things had been rearranged since my last visit. Now there was a locked file cabinet and the cabinet that Bri and I explored last week was gone. The mysterious files we had found must have been placed into a much more secure location.

Dad sat in a leather-bound office chair that swiveled slightly under his weight.

"Take a seat," he said.

After grabbing a folding metal chair and fidgeting with it for a moment, I sat. Dad and I faced each other in silence for a minute, and I wondered if I was about to be grounded.

"Son, did you see how mad your mom was?" Dad asked. "You better have a good reason as to why you needed to talk to me in private."

"I'm sorry," I said. "I don't want to make any of you upset. Something just came up." I picked up my backpack and placed it on my lap. "So, there were these tests that went missing, and then they just landed on my desk." I pulled out the tests and placed them in front of him.

Dad uttered a curse under his breath. He stood and gripped the tests tighter in one hand. As he paced the room, he slapped the tests against his hand.

"You shouldn't have these!" Dad yelled. "I'll take care of them. I have..." he paused.

"You have what, Dad?" I asked. "You can tell me. I'm off the case, remember?"

"Nice try, kiddo," he said. "I'm forbidding you and your team to go further into this investigation.

"But—"

"Good night, Marcus," Dad interrupted. He yanked the door open.

Grabbing my bag, I kept my head down as I exited the room. Once at the steps, I looked back to see Dad grimace as he closed the door to his office. In response, I swung the bag over my shoulder and stomped up the steps. On the second floor, I brushed past Bri. She was laughing and pointing at me, but I wasn't even listening. When she came toward me, I slammed the door in her face. Now, I understood why she slammed the door all the time. The action felt oddly satisfying, but only for a moment.

I tossed my bag on the floor and threw myself into bed. Looking up at the ceiling, I resolved to avoid doing homework for a moment. Instead, I took out my cell phone to text Alissa. We decided to meet outside at one o'clock in the morning. By then, everyone should be asleep. Until then, I needed to get some schoolwork done.

I spotted Alissa standing sitting on the back stoop of the house, her breath making vapors as she hugged her parka tighter.

She looked up and grinned as I approached. "This'll have to be fast. It's cold out here."

I wore a sweatshirt for warmth, so the reminder wasn't needed.

"So, Dad's up to something shady," I said as I plopped myself beside Alissa, close enough to share each other's warmth.

"What do you think?" Alissa asked.

"He's my dad," I said, propping my legs up and crossing my arms over my knees. "I think...

whatever he's involved in, we've served his purposes."

"Okay," Alissa sighed. "We'll tell the team tomorrow."

"But that doesn't mean I'm not curious about that tunnel," I added quickly.

Alissa bumped against me. "Marc, are we in or out?"

I rested my chin on my arms. "Let's research the tunnel and see what Derrick thinks Abby is up to. We'll stay clear of my dad for right now."

Alissa chuckled. "Okay. Glad we're on the same page."

We hung out for a moment longer before calling it a night due to the penetrating cold. Though I thought I'd made the right call, I couldn't help but wonder what Dad would've gotten himself into that was so dangerous.

Chapter Twenty-Three

Marcus

"There were colonial spies here!" Nate exclaimed, tapping the steering wheel of the Jeep as he drove. "They were right beneath our town."

"Yeah, that is pretty crazy," I agreed.

I couldn't believe what we learned while at the library after school today. History books showed that the more urbanized area of our town was once a hotbed of activity during the revolutionary war. Colonial spies used a network of underground tunnels to escape British soldiers. While most of the tunnels had been sealed off, several were later used to hide slaves escaping to freedom.

Nate and I were fascinated with the information to the point that we went overtime on our research. Now, we were racing the clock to get to the County Public Archives building before it closed at four o'clock this afternoon.

"Step on it, Nate," I said. "The county clerk Mrs. Addison will need to leave in 30 minutes."

"I know," Nate said.

Nate accelerated the Jeep, pushing us through a yellow light before it turned red. He continued his conversation on a fictitious scenario in which he and I played cloak and dagger while evading the grasps of a British General. I only half listened as I looked out the window at the historic buildings. The three-story buildings stood the tallest. I wondered how many tunnels we'd see buried beneath this town when Mrs. Addison pulled up the town's infrastructure maps.

A minute before four o'clock, Nate pulled up to the curb of the Public Archives. Slamming the doors shut and dropping a few coins into the meter, we raced to the front door. Though we still had just under thirty minutes to spare, there was no doubt someone would hold up the security line, or someone else would be peeved that we'd be keeping them from leaving on time.

We slowed down at the front doors and took a second to catch our breaths. Opening the door, we were greeted by an aging security guard who seemed to look past us as he stood.

"How can I help you young men?" he asked.

"We're here to see the county clerk Mrs. Jennifer Addison," Nate blurted out.

The guard frowned. "Where are your parents?"

"It's for a school project," I said. "She's expecting us."

"All right let me call up," the guard said. "We

can't have just anyone coming in here claiming to know so-and-so."

He hobbled over to a phone mounted on the wall where he picked up a receiver. Keeping his eye on us, he dialed the number and waited for someone on the other end to pick up the phone. He nodded a few times into the receiver. After hanging it up, he hobbled back to us.

"Right through this metal detector," he said. "Make sure you empty out your pockets and place them in this here tray. It'll be the fifth door on the right."

We did as we were told and placed the trays on a table before we went through a metal detector. Fortunately, neither of us set off an alarm.

Stuffing our things back into our pockets, we thanked him and scurried down the empty hallway. As the guard directed us, we found the fifth door on the right wide open with its light on. There were three metal folding chairs on the right as we entered. A half-counter lined the other end of the room. Beyond the counter, a door opened into what appeared to be an endless hallway lined with shelves.

"Do you see anyone?" I asked Nate.

"Let me try this," Nate said.

He strode up to the counter where he tapped his hand upon a bell, causing it to chime a few times.

"Be out in a minute," a woman said from the closet beyond the hallway.

The silhouette of a woman appeared in what I now realized was an archway that led down another hallway. Exiting the archway and entering the room, she offered a smile that caused crow's feet to appear around her eyes.

"You must be Marcus and Nate," she said. She looked from Nate to me. "I'm Jennifer Addison."

We exchanged pleasantries. She shook hands quickly with Nate, then wiped her palm on her dark skirt sprinkled with dust.

"I must look a mess," she said, indicating her skirt. "I've been in the back tidying up the place. Tell me about those records you're looking for?"

"We're researching the tunnel system in town," Nate said.

"Especially around the neighborhood where The Genesee Country Club is located," I added. "It's for school."

"It makes no difference to me whether you're here for a school assignment," said Mrs. Addison. Her eyes lit up. "I'm just excited to see so many people interested in the tunnels. Someone else came here asking for the same thing. Now, let's get you signed in."

She pointed to a clipboard on the counter. Nate pulled it toward him, examined it for a moment, and signed us in.

"All set," Nate said. "How much time do we have?"

"Fifteen minutes," Mrs. Addison said. "Right this way. I'll lead you to it."

I followed Mrs. Addison down the narrow corridor with Nate right behind me. The deeper we went, the more my earlier observation was confirmed that a hallway existed as she took a right, then a left.

"This is like the Tardis!" Nate exclaimed. "Does

this ever end?"

"Here we are," Mrs. Addison said. She stopped at an open drawer. "As you can see, I'd just begun my search when I heard someone ring the bell." She eyed Nate.

"Sorry, that was me," he said. Nate scratched the back of his neck and raised his hand.

"I know," Mrs. Addison said.

She lifted her glasses from around her neck and adjusted them, so they would rest just at the bridge of her nose. She began to dig through the files.

"Now, I can't let you take these out of this room, which is why I didn't bring them up to you." Mrs. Addison said. "But there's a pull-out counter here you can use to do your research." She hunched over the files, fingering through one after another. "Ah! Here's the file. It was stuck between a few others. My last visitor must've put it in wrong." She straightened up and reached for a handle sitting chest high. "If you boys would step back."

Without waiting, she positioned herself between us and pulled the handle. Nate and I repositioned ourselves with a duck and a shuffle as a short counter slid out. Mrs. Addison slapped down a thick file on the counter.

"You boys have ten minutes," she said. "Now, if you'll excuse me."

Nate plastered himself against the wall as Mrs. Addison brushed past him. Seeing nowhere else for me to go, I headed back toward the office with Mrs. Addison right behind me. The first corner we came to provided enough room for Mrs.

Anderson to squeeze by, though not without some displeasure on her part.

"Thanks again," I said to her back.

"Don't mention it," she said without turning around. "Nine minutes."

I returned to the counter where Nate had already gone through multiple documents.

"Did you get a good look at the name on the clipboard?" I asked when I approached. Nate flipped over another page, scanned it onto his phone, then moved on.

"It's a girl's handwriting," he said. "She signed as Ralph Rotten."

One after another, Nate pulled out large documents containing a crisscrossing maze of lines and numbers. These he scanned it into his app, then flipped the page over.

"Bro, this is kind of therapeutic," Nate said.

"With all that scanning you're doing, I hope you found something," I said.

"We'll have to study them more closely when we get to a computer. I'm sure we'll figure something...wait!"

"What is it?"

I stepped over to the counter and examined the document. Nate grabbed the stack he'd already scanned, quickly flipped through them, and laid them down.

"It's not here," Nate said. "The two-block radius around the Genesee seems to be missing."

"We should bring it up to Mrs. Addison," I said. "If we don't, she'll think we took it."

Nate resorted the papers back into the folder. "Good idea. Let's do that."

We carefully maneuvered our way through the narrow hallway to avoid the extended drawer handles. Upon entering Mrs. Addison's office, I saw she was seated in one of the folding metal chairs, her eyes glued to her watch. She looked up.

"There you are," she said cheerfully. "But you weren't supposed to bring the files."

"I know," I said. "But we wanted to let you know one of the files is missing."

She stood. "Oh, dear! Let me see that." She grabbed the folder out of Nate's hands. "Thanks. You boys should head out. I'm sure it's just a filing error."

After thanking her and wishing her a good evening, Nate and I headed into the lobby where the security guard was already waiting by the door. When we approached, he released us into the frigid late afternoon air, then locked the door behind us.

Once a safe distance away from the Public Archives Building, I gave voice to my thoughts.

"So, I can see why we would want part of the map, but why would someone else want it?" I asked.

"I don't know," Nate said with steel in his voice. "Mrs. Addison did say someone came in before us. Maybe they had something to do with the map disappearance." He opened the driver's side door of the Jeep. "Hop in. Janice said to meet them in the food court, and I'm getting kinda hungry. Let's see what they found out."

I climbed into the Jeep. Before I could fasten my seatbelt, Nate revved the engine and pulled away from the parking spot. I quickly put on my seatbelt and intentionally clicked it, so Nate could hear. He glanced my way.

"Sorry, I didn't realize you hadn't buckled up. We just needed to get away from there."

"Why?" I asked.

Nate checked his mirrors. "Just on the lookout, you know?"

I checked my mirrors as well and wondered if Nate could be capable of stealing a government document. His behavior changed as he seemed edgy. The possibility that someone could come after us might have scared him. Before our trip, I felt confident, but now I felt like we were being followed. I needed to be alert.

Chapter Twenty-Four

Alissa

Janice and I sat across from Abby and Mel at the food court. Abby and Janice both had a Caesar salad and grilled chicken on their trays while Mel and I had opted for the greasier Chinese food to get the full mall food experience.

"It's been so cool hanging out with you girls," Abby said between bites of food.

"I know," Janice said. "We should've done this a long time ago."

Abby nodded and looked between Mel and me. "When we're done here, you two should totally get something for yourselves. I feel like I'm the only one buying anything."

I glanced at several bags labeled with designer logos at Abby's feet. I knew Janice saw the bags, too.

"I bought a couple of things," she said

defensively.

"From one store," Abby said. "Janice, I think our super, sporty friends Mel and Alissa here could use a little fashion makeover."

"I don't know," I said.

"Oh, come on," said Abby. "It'll be fun. We can go...uh-oh." Abby shrank in her seat. "Hide me."

"What's wrong, Abs?" asked Mel as she chewed her rice from General Tso's chicken.

Janice and I looked around the food court. I didn't see anything off. Then, I heard him.

"Hey, Abby!" Derrick called out as he walked closer. "I didn't know you'd be here."

"Surprise," Abby said through clenched teeth as she turned in his direction.

Derrick tilted his head. "But I thought you were—"

"I'm here now." Abby stood and turned her back to him. "Sorry, girls. Give me a minute."

Abby mouthed the words help me and turned back to Derrick. When she reached him, she took Derrick by the arm and led him away from the table. Mel sighed.

"Can I get a ride home?" she asked.

"Why would you need a ride home?" I asked.

"Just wait."

The three of us sat quietly at the table. A few seconds went by and then the shouting began.

"Stalker much!" Abby yelled.

"You're overreacting!" Derrick yelled back.

A few heads turned in the food court as Derrick and Abby loudly exchanged a few choice words.

"And that's why I need a ride," Mel said.

"You can ride with Alissa me," Janice said. She

looked to me eagerly. "Right, Lis?"

Her grin let me know she had some ulterior motives. I wasn't sure what she wanted to do, but I decided to go with it. I forced a smile while my phone buzzed. When I checked my notifications, I saw Marcus had texted me that he and Nate were here.

"You can come with us, Mel," I said. "It's no problem. We just need to talk to Marcus and Nate first. They should be meeting us right about now." I glanced over Mel's shoulder and spotted the boys. "Speaking of which, here they are now."

I waved them over. Nate waved back, but Marcus didn't. His posture appeared rigid. Marcus exercised regularly, especially with all the sports he played, so I wasn't sure why he looked so stiff. When they spotted Derrick and Abby in their screaming match, they tip-toed by them and walked faster to us.

"Looks like Derrick didn't need us after all," Nate said as he approached Janice and wrapped his arms around her.

"Need him for what?" Mel questioned.

"Uh...nothing." Nate laughed anxiously. "Anyway, Marcus and I found some really cool stuff. Ain't that right, Marcus?" Nate looked expectantly to Marcus, who narrowed his eyes at him.

I could feel the tension. I wasn't sure what happened on their car ride over here, but I didn't like Marcus's behavior.

"Marcus, are you going to answer Nate's question?" I asked.

"Maybe later," Marcus replied coolly, still not taking his eyes off Nate. "I just have a lot on my mind right now."

"Awkward," Mel said. She looked to Janice and me. "I'm getting some seriously weird vibes. If you want, I can just take a Lyft home. I don't want any drama."

"No, it's fine," I replied. "We'll take you." I glared at Marcus. "And you...we'll talk later when we meet at the usual spot later. But before then, just be nice to Nate."

"Yeah, Marcus, be nice," Janice chimed in. "Douchebag doesn't suit you."

Nate snickered while Marcus sighed.

As Mel, Janice, and I headed in opposite directions of Marcus and Nate, I couldn't help but wonder what happened to them. They had been boys since way back. Whatever had gotten between them must've been pretty serious.

The girls and I headed to my car, so we could take Mel home. Per usual, Janice messed with the radio. As I drove, I took a glance in my rearview mirror and noticed Mel with her eyes on me.

"What's up?" I asked. "You look like you want to say something."

"You all think you've got it all figured out," she said slyly. "Don't think I don't see you trying to cozy up to Abby."

In the corner of my eye, Janice froze. She took her hand off the dial and slowly eased back into the passenger's seat. I chewed my inner cheek but continued to look ahead of me.

"Alissa don't look so surprised," Mel said. "I've been telling you all along. Whatever you're trying to do, you need to back off. Abby doesn't let just anyone in. Neither does her family." She scooted up in the back seat. "I've been at this a lot longer than you. I deserve this!"

"Umm...Mel, what the heck are you talking?" Janice asked.

"You still don't get it?" Mel asked. "Everyone knows how you four exposed last semester's financial scandal. Most people know about what happened last summer — not that I care."

As she waited us out, my mind raced. Except for getting caught skipping school, we'd been careful. I wondered how she could possibly know that we were onto Abby's suspicious acceptance into Penamore College. Even though I wanted to ask Mel, I remained hesitant. Janice groaned and turned to Mel in the back seat.

"Say what you've gotta say," Janice demanded.

My mouth dropped. I'd never heard Janice sound this serious, but Mel seemed unfazed.

"So, you wanna know what's on my mind?" she asked. She leaned forward and rested her arms on our seats. "Okay, here it is. Abby doesn't like being stalked, okay? What did you all do?"

"Fine," I said flatly. "I'll tell you. Derrick approached Marcus and Nate. He thought Abby was cheating on him."

"Is that all?" Mel asked. She relaxed and scooted back to her seat.

"That's crazy, right?" Janice asked. She laughed. "Boys can be so stupid sometimes."

"Well, he we are," I said. I pulled my car up to the curb.

Mel sat back and unfasten her seatbelt. As she grabbed the door handle, she seemed to avoid my gaze through the rearview mirror.

"Thanks for the ride...and everything," she said simply. She closed the door and walked up to Janice on the passenger's side.

Janice and I shared a mutual glance. Mel didn't budge, so Janice slowly lowered her window.

"Did you forget something?" she asked.

"No, it's not that," replied Mel. "If Derrick still wants you to follow Abby, you probably shouldn't do it on Saturday."

"What's going on Saturday?" I asked.

Mel winked. "There's a big event happening at the Genesee. Abby and her family are going. I'll be working there all day by the way. I just thought you should know. See you all tomorrow." She walked to her front door and headed inside. Janice rolled up the window and turned toward me.

"Was that weird or what?" asked Janice.

"I don't know," I said. "Not sure if she's onto us, baiting us, or both."

Janice nodded. "I vote both. This probably isn't the first time Derrick tried something like this on Abby. And Mel definitely has something to gain or lose in whatever she's involved in."

I took a deep breath. "So, what do we do about it?"

"Well," Janice said. "We've got some tunnels to look into. Maybe that'll keep us underground for a while at least until Saturday."

"That works for me." I put the car into drive. "Now that we're done here, let's meet the boys."

Chapter Twenty-Five

Alissa

By the time Janice and I arrived at Slices, our conversation had already shifted toward the weird vibe we'd gotten from Marcus and Nate at the mall. When we entered, they sat at a table in the back corner of the restaurant, facing the entrance. When we approached the table, Marcus stood.

"Alissa, you look tense," he said as he stepped toward me.

"I'm okay now," I said. "You seem to be in a better mood."

"Now, you two look like that little drive to Mel's house was anything but pleasant," said Nate.

"We should probably sit," Janice said as she combed her fingers through her hair, a trait she'd clearly picked up from Nate.

"Right," I said as I scooted in beside Marcus. "Mel knows Derrick contracted us to follow Abby. We're also pretty sure she knows we know something shady's happening at The Genesee."

Janice went on to explain how Mel all but invited us to the country club where she happens to work.

"Maybe we're taking a flying leap here," Janice said. "But whatever is happening, we should check it out."

"But you don't know what it is," Marcus concluded.

"Right," Janice said. "I searched the Genesee's site on the way here. Nothing!"

"Which brings us to our research," Nate said. He slid his phone over to Janice. "We've gotten all but one of the tunnel maps of the area surrounding The Genesee."

Janice placed the phone between her and me on the center of the table. She swiped the screen, paused on the first map, and studied it for a minute.

"What happened to the missing map?" I asked.

"Mrs. Addison says old archives go missing all the time," Marcus said. He looked to Nate.

"No worries, though," Nate said. He reached into his coat pocket.

"Don't tell me you stole it," Janice said.

Nate paused, with his hand still in his pocket. "As tempting as that may sound, I didn't." He pulled out a pad of paper and a pen. "I thought we could sketch out each map, and maybe fill in the missing details from those."

"Hold up," Marcus said. He shook his head.

"So, you didn't steal the map?"

"No way! If I'd stolen it, you would've known by now. I share everything with you guys."

Marcus's face reddened. "Well, I feel stupid."

"Yeah, you should," I added. "Now, apologize to Nate."

"Sorry, bro," said Marcus. "I shouldn't have doubted you. It's just that you were acting super shady on the drive to the mall, so I had my doubts."

"It's all good," Nate said. "I was looking out because I thought I saw a Lexus sedan following us several car lengths back. I think it might've been Maddox."

"Do you think it was really him?" A ping came from Marcus's phone. "My bad. Let me see what this is." After Marcus unlocked his phone, he paused and looked at me.

"What is it?" I asked. I peeked at his phone and immediately scrunched my face. "It's her, isn't it? She's messaging you on my spoofed Instagram account."

"Oh, is that the other woman?" Nate asked. "Let me see! The maps can wait."

"You're getting a little too excited there," Janice said snidely.

"She says she's in a Cadillac and she's here right now," blurted Marcus.

"I think I see her out the window." Janice pointed.

We all watched as a girl, rather a young woman, waved at us as she strolled past the window of a Slices. While every part of my being told me to get out of there, curiosity seemed to keep me seated.

When the front door chimed, I kept my eyes on Nate and Janice, who watched the front entrance intently.

Clicking heels on tile flooring announced her approach. None of us turned to look. That is, not until she grated a chair across the floor and slid up to our booth. By that point, a few patrons looked to our table before they returned to their meals. I crossed my arms and waited to see what this lady wanted.

"Hey, guys!" she cheered. "It's nice to finally meet the rest of you. Marcus and I already met. It's practically our second date now."

"That's it," I said. I stood up. "You need to tell us who you are right now."

The lady gulped. "Okay, I'll cut to the chase. I hacked into your social media account to get closer to Marcus, but it was only to find out information."

"Those are some pretty good tech skills," Nate said.

"Nate, who's side are you on?" I asked.

He shrugged. "Hey, it's not my fault she got into your account. You and Marcus need to get a better handle on your social media accounts."

I scoffed and sat down. "Whatever. I didn't know my account was so valuable."

"Yes, your account is very valuable," said the woman. "Oh, where are my manners? My name's Cassie Maddox."

She extended her hand, but I didn't bother to shake it. Seeing as no one took her hand, she lowered it and cleared her throat.

"Maddox," Marcus blurted. "I know that last

name." He snapped his finger. "Are you Mr. Maddox's daughter?"

"I'm his niece," Cassie corrected Marcus. "His name is Alfred Maddox, but that doesn't matter. You guys are so close."

"Close to what?" Janice asked.

"I'd thought you'd never ask," said Cassie.

Cassie proceeded to tell us about how she'd gotten into a school for an exceptional talent in crew even though she'd never participated in the sport. While her parents told her not to worry, she still had her doubts. When she was expected to play, she dropped out before risking exposure and embarrassment. Somehow, her sudden drop out made her acceptance into community college more difficult

"I'm pretty sure my Uncle Alfred had something do with it," she said. "I haven't been able to prove anything, which is why I need your help."

The four of us exchanged looks until Janice, Nate, and I focused on Marcus. He leaned back. Then, he shrugged.

"That's all very interesting, but so what?" he asked.

"Okay, that's fair," said Cassie. "I get it. You don't know me, but maybe you're familiar with the Genesee." She pulled out a map and unfolded it. "I think we can get inside through the tunnel system."

"You stole it!" yelled Nate. "We were looking for that!" Nate grabbed the map.

"I borrowed it," Cassie corrected him. "I'm gonna return it when we're done with the case."

"You know?" I asked. I shook my head. "I can't do this. First, you waltz in here after you spoofed my account and then you flirt with Marcus. Now, you claim to be on the case. The whole thing sounds sus."

"Yeah," Janice agreed. "How can we trust you?"

Cassie looked nervously between us. Then, she sighed.

"I get it. I'm just one person who you don't know very well. I was...I mean I am really new to this. It was someone else's stupid idea. My source... he's been working this case."

"Who's your source?" Nate asked as his interest seemed to peak.

"Well, it's good to see you know where allegiance lies," I told him sarcastically.

"Sorry," Cassie said. "I really can't reveal that information."

"Then why you?" Marcus asked.

Before speaking, Cassie scratched lightly on her cheek, then looked at me. "We have a mutual friend whose acceptance to Penamore is in jeopardy."

Suddenly, Mel's warnings and little hints began to fall into place.

"I assume you mean Mel Albright," I said.

All eyes in our little group focused on Cassie who shrank back from the sudden attention. She nodded slowly, and I smiled triumphantly. Now, I felt in control.

"How do you know Mel?" I asked.

"We met at lacrosse camp a couple summers ago," said Cassie. "I was a going into my senior year and she was going into her sophomore year.

Somehow, she's been pulled into whatever all this is. Now, they've got her doing something to keep her spot at Penamore and she won't say."

I rubbed my chin. "Mel told us to stay out of it, too."

"Well, it sounds like we're all caught up," Nate added. He slid the map over to Cassie. "Now that's all settled, where do we begin?"

For the next few minutes, we discussed plans with Cassie. She suggested we explore the old tunnels in the Genesee because she'd seen her uncle use them a few times. While the others seemed to agree with her, I remained skeptical. There was no way I was about to give her a pass. Sensing my apprehension, Cassie stood. She handed me a card.

"Here's my contact info," she said. "Don't wait too long to get in touch."

We watched as Cassie walked out the restaurant and returned to her car without giving us a second look even as she passed the window. I did a double take when I finally examined her card and passed it to Marcus.

"Whoa!" he exclaimed. "She's a P.I."

"Yes, that may be true," I said as I snatched the card back, "but I still don't trust her."

"Agreed," Janice said. "How about you, Nate?"

"I say we play along for now," Nate said. "We'll tell her we'll get back to her on Saturday morning." He gestured for us to lean in, so we did. "But while we wait, hear me out. I have an idea."

Chapter Twenty-Six

Marcus

When we pulled into our neighborhood that evening, Dad was standing on the front porch. Even in the distance, I could make out his breath, a puff of mist in the cold, night air. As Alissa pulled into her driveway, I glimpsed Bri peeking out the window through the curtains. When she and I locked eyes, she let the curtain drop. Alissa parked and turned off her car engine. While we unbuckled our seatbelts, I noticed Dad approaching us. I sighed and Alissa grabbed my hand.

"Are we good?" she asked.

"I hope so," I replied.

We got out the car and Dad stopped a few feet from us.

"Now, where have you two been?" Dad asked.

"We were hanging at Slices with Nate and Janice," I said as I shut the car door.

"Working on the case I'm sure." He gave a crooked smile. "You can't fool me. What did you find?"

"Well, since we're sharing, what did you find, Dad?" I asked. I crossed my arms and waited for him to spill some information.

"Let's have a seat," Dad said.

He turned toward the porch, so Alissa and I followed him. When we reached the porch, we each took a seat on mock wicker furniture, winter ready and bare of all cushioning. Dad gazed into the darkness beyond the porch light. I hadn't seen him this quiet in a while, so I hoped whatever he had to say wasn't bad. He rubbed his hands together and looked our direction.

"It's like this," Dad said. "When I returned in December and took on the administrative duties, I noticed some discrepancies, not all of which were a result of someone skimming off the top of the booster club funds. There was something else. If you hadn't noticed, Principal Moss hasn't been exactly present lately."

"I hadn't," Alissa said. "But by the way, he gave Janice and me detention, but Mel and Abby didn't get it. Why is that?"

Dad cocked an eyebrow. "I was getting to that. Like I was saying, Moss has been noticeably absent. The secretary keeps immaculate records of his appointments, including those appointments labeled 'Legacy' and those labeled out of office. Upon further inspection, since the information was public, I noticed that whenever a Legacy appointment occurred, an out of office appointment would immediately follow often with the same participants from the Legacy appointment." He paused and looked between us. "The day of Alissa's excursion with Janice happened to follow the day after Moss had met with Abby's parents. That appointment also happened to be a Legacy."

My breath caught in my throat while Alissa's eyes widened. We realized the connection, though obvious, was circumstantial at best. Alissa forced a laugh.

"Okay, Abby's parents had a Legacy appointment, but Mel's parents weren't there," Alissa said casually. "That still doesn't seem like enough reason for both Abby and Mel not to get detention."

"Moss insisted they'd done no wrong," Dad replied.

"Maybe Mel knew something about that guy we saw her with the other night," I added. I pondered for a moment. "Dad, can you tell us about the guy who was hanging in our driveway the other night?"

"Sure, I'll tell you," Dad said. "Here, catch this." He tossed me a card.

I caught the card easily. I flipped it over and read it.

Dylan Maddox, Lenape County Sherriff

"What's wrong, Marc?" Alissa asked. "Why do you look like that?"

I handed the card to Alissa. She gasped and let the card slip from her hands. I reached to grab it before it hit the ground, but Dad didn't seem to notice. He was back to looking at the night sky.

"We got all that evidence for nothing," said Dad. "Sheriff Maddox said there was nothing he can do. 'Circumstantial,' he said. But he assured me that I made the report in good faith."

"That's it?" Alissa asked.

Dad shook his head and got up. "I'm afraid so. That's why I put an end to all of this. What can an assistant principal and four kids do against all that?"

Alissa nudged me. "Are you going to tell him?"

"Tell me what?" Dad asked.

"Nothing," I said as I laughed. "It's been a long day. You know how it is."

Dad narrowed his eyes. "Yeah, I do. Let me know if there's anything else. I'm a knock or a phone call away. Good night. Don't stay out too long. It's cold out here."

As Dad opened the door and stepped inside, Bri peeked out through the curtains again. Alissa waved, and Bri made a mean face before she moved from the curtain. After my dad latched the front door shut, Alissa grabbed me.

"So, now we have two Maddoxes to worry about," she said. "Alfred Maddox, Cassie's uncle and Sheriff Dylan Maddox."

"My head hurts," I said. I slouched in the chair. "All of this is starting to sound like a set-up."

"All of it is super convenient," Alissa said. "Whatever it is." Her phone buzzed and she shook her head. "It's my mom. I forgot to tell my mom I was on my way home. Let's meet later tonight. Gotta go!" Alissa skipped off the porch and darted across our driveways.

I watched her go and wondered if we were indeed being set up. Knowing the possibility was one thing and being prepared for it was the other. Still, we'd gone this far. Whatever secrets lay within that tunnel and beyond the doors of The Genesee Country Club were way too big to leave alone.

Alissa stopped at the door and waved to me. I waved back. Or maybe those secrets were way too big to not leave alone. Either way, someone in the Sherriff's department had evidence big enough for someone else to investigate.

That night long after Dad gave me another warning, I lay awake, periodically checking my phone as if one-thirty in the morning would come any sooner. When the text came through from Alissa to meet, I popped out of bed fully dressed except for my shoes. I slipped on my shoes by my bed and grabbed my tactical pen. There was no way I'd leave without it, not after what I'd seen Nate could do to a guy.

I popped open my door and crept down the hallway. I briefly stopped at my parents' door to make sure they were asleep. The telltale signs of Dad's snoring and Mom's light slumber let me know I could continue to walk.

Now, I only had to pass Bri's door undetected. She couldn't follow me. I placed my ear to her door. On the other side of the door, the bed creaked. Satisfied she was still in her room, I descended the steps and skipped the fifth one that would most assuredly give me away.

Once on the first floor, I grabbed my coat from

the rack. Opening the door to the frigid air, I shivered and stepped through the door. As I closed the door quickly behind me, a shadowy figure formed at the top of the steps. My heart raced as I threw on my jacket. In my periphery, I spotted Alissa, darting down the sidewalk. I caught up with her.

"Did anyone see you?" she asked.

I momentarily visualized the shadow at the top of the steps that seemed to watch me leave, but I decided not to tell Alissa about it.

"I escaped without a trace," I lied.

"That may be so," Alissa said, "but I'm the queen of stealth." She grinned.

"Well, queen, they're waiting."

We jogged two blocks until we came to Nate's Jeep. With the lights off and the engine running, he didn't appear to look like he was trying to be inconspicuous. When the lights flashed twice, Alissa and I darted into the shadows until we popped open the rear passenger doors on either side of the Jeep.

"You two are the worst spies ever," Nate said.

"They are not," said Janice as she slapped him playfully.

"Doesn't matter," I said. "Let's go."

I glanced out the window. Shadows of leafless trees danced upon the walkway and neighborhood road. Their movement messed with my eyes, giving me the feeling someone was following us.

Easing on the gas, Nate guided the Jeep through the neighborhood. From the front seat, Janice turned and handed square, plastic disks to

Alissa and me.

"What are these?" I asked.

"They're trackers, and Janice and I have the app on our phones," Nate said. "If something happens to one of us, these little guys will track our location."

"What if something happens to you and Janice?" I asked.

Nate groaned. "Bro, we go in pairs. That's what we always do. Janice or I will stay back with one of you."

When Nate guided the Jeep onto the main road, he flipped the lights on and gunned the engine. I looked back. The shadows had faded. Feeling satisfied no one followed us, I allowed myself to relax.

We filled Janice and Nate in on Dad's failed attempt to work with Sheriff Dylan Maddox and our suspicion that Cassie, the detective, may be the sheriff's daughter.

"That's an interesting hunch," Janice said.

"Yeah, and it's all the more reason we need to keep a GPS tracker on each of us," said Nate.

As Nate pulled onto the highway, the Jeep picked up speed. Nate and Janice acted like we were simply headed out for a fun night Beside me, Alissa stiffened. I placed my arm around her and pulled her close. Whatever we were doing, I knew Alissa and I shared the same sentiment. Something didn't feel right.

Chapter Twenty-Seven

Alissa

"It should be right around here," Marcus said, stopping midway through an alleyway.

Marcus adjusted the camera strapped over his shoulder. The camera, a bulky object, seemed unnecessary since we had phones. But Nate and Janice made a compelling case about the potential of needing to go dark.

"All right let's get some light," he said.

I pulled out my tactical pen and flipped the switch, illuminating the walls around us. Somewhere around here Cassie had insisted her uncle Alfred Maddox had managed to duck into a secret passageway. I still wondered why she, specifically, had been following him since her father Dylan Maddox was a detective. All the more reason why I didn't trust her, even though she was still our best lead.

"Can you shine your light over here?" Marcus asked.

"You know you have your own, right?" I asked.

"Yeah, but I wanted to share yours." He adjusted the map.

I smiled and obliged as I walked over to him with my tactical pen. "You're such a dork. Let's see what we have."

Janice's detailed map indicated we stood near intersecting alleyways. Somewhere beneath us there began a network of tunnels. Since Cassie wasn't clear on where her uncle managed to duck into a secret passageway, Marcus and I were tasked with checking every wall around this area for a hidden entrance. I shifted the light along down the alleyway.

"You'll need your own light for this part, Marcus," I suggested.

Marcus tucked the map away and pulled out his tactical pen. He touched the walls to feel for any sign of an entrance. I did the same on my side as I ran my fingers over cold, damp brick. In my coat pocket, the walkie-talkie Janice had handed to me when we were back in the Jeep clicked. I pulled it out.

"Are you guys okay?" Nate asked as his voice crackled through the walkie-talkie. "You've been standing there for a while."

"Yeah, Nate," I said as I clicked the talk button. "We're looking for an entrance. It's not that easy."

"Right," Marcus agreed as he walked over to me. "Nate must think it'll just pop out."

"Okay, my bad," said Nate over the walkie-talkie. "Remember overwatch has your back. Over."

I stuffed the walkie back into my pocket and shook my head.

"Marc, this is fun and all, but I think we should head back if we don't find anything soon," I said.

In the distance, a bottle clanked and crashed. Then came the hollow thud and bang of a dumpster. Marcus turned and beamed his flashlight in the direction of the noise. A cat screeched, which caused us both to jump.

"Yeah, it's time to go," Marcus said.

"We should keep moving," I said. A chill penetrated through my jacket.

Shining his light ahead of us, Marcus lead the way. He adjusted the camera on his shoulder.

As we walked on, I thought of Nate and Janice huddled nice and warm in the Jeep where we parked it several blocks away. Far enough not to draw attention to our location, but close enough should we need to evade getting caught by looping back around some other way.

Above us, a light mounted on the corner of the building flickered and cracked. The three-way intersecting alleyway illuminated with an eerie glow that made everything around us seem almost alive. We came to the T on the map and a wall lined with two rusty dumpsters, one twice the size of the other. Next to the larger dumpster, someone had piled up several bags of trash. A rat skittered across the pavement and slithered beneath the smaller dumpster. I stopped and Marcus halted.

"I'm not going down either one of these side streets," I said firmly. I imagined a hidden camera accompanying the flickering light above us. "I'm beginning to think our friend Cassie is just messing with us."

"I hear ya, Lis, but we've come so far," Marcus said. He continued to scan the area of pavement and walls until his light came to a stop on the smaller dumpster. "Help me move this."

Marcus took a step toward the dumpster and I joined him. I took one side of the dumpster while Marcus took the other. I popped the wheel lock out of place and stood.

"What are you expecting to find behind these anyway?" I asked. "We already know at least one rat lives under here."

"I don't know," Marcus said. From the other side, he popped his wheel lock, causing a metallic thud. "Maybe we'll get lucky and find a hidden door."

"I wouldn't be surprised if we did, seeing as a hidden door in the country club led us to a secret tunnel."

"Are you ready to see what's behind the dumpster?" Marcus smiled mischievously. "As the saying goes, one man's trash is another man's treasure."

I clicked my teeth. "Yeah, whatever. Let's just move this thing. We'll push away from the wall on three."

In a quick three count, the dumpster moved. It rattled and rolled in my direction.

"Alissa, watch out!" Marcus yelled.

Fortunately, I jumped out the way to avoid the

dumpster, which slammed into the corner of the building. If I had moved a second slower, I was positive my toes would've been crushed.

"Alissa, are you okay?" Marcus asked as he rushed to my side. "I was worried."

"I'm good," I said. I winked. "I think I can handle a runaway dumpster."

Marcus blew a sigh of relief. "That may be so, but I think I'll handle this next dumpster."

Marcus turned and slid his fingers between the wall and the corner of the dumpster. He struggled to pull, and something metallic seemed to shift.

"It's not moving," Marcus said.

"I don't think it's supposed to," I said. "But something else is. Do that again."

Marcus sighed. "Now, who's messing around?"

Marcus returned to the dumpster. He fit his fingers once again between the corner of the dumpster and the wall. He pulled. I listened, and nothing happened. I drew my attention to Marcus.

"Try positioning your hands differently," I said.

Marcus did as I suggested, but nothing budged. He stepped out the way.

"Do you want to try?" Marcus asked.

I took his place. If my hunch was right, there'd be something. I slid my fingers behind the dumpster to feel for a lever that would have to squeeze in just the right place. At first, I felt nothing but solid, smooth metal where Marcus had pulled. Sliding my fingers slowly up and down the back of the dumpster, I felt the smallest crease. I shifted both my hands up and squeezed. Behind me, something metallic shifted once again.

"You've got to be kidding," Marcus said.

Marcus pointed to the ground. As the storm drain slid and scraped with metallic protest, two rats climbed out of the drain and scurried down the alleyway. When the grate opened fully, I released the lever and stared at the hole in the ground.

"Just like old times!" I exclaimed.

"I'll take the basement of a run-down cabin over this any day of the week," Marcus said.

I narrowed my eyes. "Marcus Kahale are you saying you're afraid to explore some tunnels?"

"Heck no!" Marcus paused and looked around. "Let's just let overwatch know what we've found first."

I pulled out the walkie and clicked talk. "Overwatch, this is team KC. Are you there?"

Glancing at Marcus, I couldn't help but notice his crooked grin. Even in the shadows of a flickering light, his eyes still seemed to twinkle with mischief. I clicked the talk button again.

"Overwatch, come in," I repeated.

"Sorry," Janice said over the walkie-talkie. "Uh, go ahead."

"We found a tunnel. Marcus is taking a picture right now and sending it to Nate. We're going in."

Janice paused. "Uh...ten-four. Be careful."

I stuffed the walkie back in my pocket. "Took them long enough to respond."

Marcus headed over to the rolling dumpster and grabbed the far corner that had hit the wall.

"We should move this back in place," Marcus said.

"Right," I said and took the other corner.

We pushed the dumpster until we lined it up against the open storm drain. After locking the wheels into place, Marcus shined his flashlight down the hole.

"There's a ladder," Marcus said. "I'm going to go down and see if there's a way to close the grate from below."

"I'll wait here, then," I said.

Marcus descended into the hole. As soon as his head was below ground level, the grate began to shut. I grabbed the lever behind the dumpster and squeezed. The grate didn't reverse directions.

"Hold up," I said.

"What's going on?" Marcus asked.

"I don't know," I said. "Just sit tight."

A moment later, the grate closed. I tried the lever again, but nothing happened. Marcus's light danced around the storm drain.

"It might be on a timer," said Marcus. "I don't see anything down here to reopen the grate." Banging echoed from the storm drain.

"What do you propose we do?" I asked.

"Wait there," Marcus said. "Call Nate and Janice. You guys keep a lookout, and I'll explore down here."

"What if you can't get out?"

He paused and scuffled. "I'll find a way out. I've got a map."

"Okay, let me give you this just in case." I fished around my pocket and found the key from the tunnel into the Country Club. "Take this."

I slid the key through the grate. Marcus grabbed the key and our hands touched.

"Just be careful, okay?" I asked.

"I will," Marcus replied. He walked away but stopped. "Love you."

"I love you, too," I said.

Marcus disappeared and his light slowly fading until it was no more. Somewhere down the alleyway, another bottle clanked, followed by something skidding across the concrete. I waited and grabbed my walkie.

"Overwatch, come in," I said.

Behind me, the dumpster shifted. Footsteps from around the dumpster shuffled. Suddenly, I had a sinking feeling. We'd been followed and we'd missed it. The dumpster began to move. I gripped my tactical pen and wondered if it would be enough to ward off an attack. My eyes darted to the wheel lock. In one movement, I kicked it and shoved the dumpster. Then, I bolted.

Chapter Twenty-Eight

Marcus

My head seemed to spin as I took slow steady steps down the tunnel. Alissa said she loved me. Though I knew it along, hearing her say those three words seemed to make it more real. I grinned. My heart still raced as I rounded another corner.

Something scampered in my surroundings. As I spun, the glow of the flashlight darted across the walls, which shimmered with the dampness. Then, I saw it. My light radiated a beady glow back to me. More rats.

This would've been a whole lot better had Alissa been able to come down here with me. Even better had I been able to meet up with the whole team. Then I remembered. Alissa was the only one with a walkie-talkie. I pulled out my phone. Hitting the home screen revealed what I'd already known. With no signal down here, no one would be able to track me.

I picked up the pace. I needed to get to an access point where my pocket GPS and my phone would be able to pick up a signal. According to the map I held, I still had a few hundred yards to go before I would be able to shift from a crouching position in the storm drain tunnel to a standing position. I needed to find that access point soon.

With every step I took, my footsteps echoed with splashing. If anyone was in pursuit, I don't know if I would have been able to pick up the second, or even third set of footsteps. I stopped. Around me the splashing died down. I circled the area with my flashlight, illuminating everything around me, before I continued my trek.

Another hundred yards with no indication of company beyond stale water and water rats, I came to a steel access door. To my disappointment, it looked super modern. Somehow, I'd expected an ancient wooden door engraved with masonic symbols. Taking a deep breath, I grabbed the handle of the steel door and pulled. Unlike the faux dumpster above ground, this door appeared to serve a purpose. Namely, to keep people out. I grunted and strained. Around me, the tunnel echoed with creaking exertion until I felt a sudden give. I flew backwards and landed in frigid water that stank of rot and filth. By my side, the camera bag lay in the water. I grabbed it up just as a rat scurried over my leg. Jumping to my feet, I swiped at the rat and sent it sailing across the tunnel floor. When it landed, it stood on hind legs, hissed, and ran off.

Alone once again, I pulled out my tactical pen, clicked the light on, and focused it on the passageway before me. To my delight, an ancient wooden door greeted me. Coming closer, I recognized the eye in the center of a triangle.

"Jackpot," I whispered. I lightly clasped my hands together and wished Alissa or Nate were here to celebrate this momentous occasion. Then, I remembered the camera. I pulled it out, examined it quickly for damage, and turned it on. I took a few shots of the tunnel, the tunnel leading to the door, and the door itself.

Securing the camera, I examined the door closer and wondered how I might get inside. I spotted an ancient keyhole and wondered if the key Alissa had given me would fit. I pulled out the key and examined it. The tip of the key appeared to be the same shape of the keyhole. I imagined others before me using this very same key to access this very same door. Holding my breath, I inserted the key. It fit easily. Stealing another glance around me, I turned the key. The lock clicked and popped open.

As I pushed the door open, a cold stale gust of air hit me in the face. Shining the light into this part of the tunnel, I was glad to see that it was at least dry. Stepping over the threshold, I stopped. Somewhere in the tunnel, water splashed. I stuffed the key back in my pocket, secured the strap on the camera bag, and grabbed the metal door. As I pulled, the door gave with grinding on mental until it closed me in. Just me and this new tunnel illuminated by a pocket-sized light.

Once again, I pulled out the map. Somewhere up ahead, the tunnel branched off to the right, toward The Genesee. If I was to find my way out of this tunnel, that's where I needed to go. Alissa and Janice said a tunnel ran between The Genesee and what seemed to serve as some off-site interrogation center. At least, that's the conclusion Alissa and Janice drew when they overheard the conversation between Mel, Abby, and a couple of adults.

As I trekked on, I noticed a steady decline in the tunnel. This access point was taking me deeper into the heart of the city. I imagined finding some secret hideout where colonial patriots planned an assault on British soldiers. Then I realized it must be getting late. I turned on my phone, confirming my fears. It was past three o'clock in the morning. Behind me, something metallic creaked that sent an echo through the tunnel. I'd been followed. This I knew for certain. I picked up the pace until I hung a right at an intersection. Just beyond me, a faint glow illuminated from the wall.

I slowed to check my phone once again while simultaneously keeping my tactical pen trained in front of me for self-defense.

I still have no bars, I thought.

I stuffed my phone back in my pocket. Eventually it would be of use to me. I only hoped I could use it soon. In the back of my mind, I knew my friends had my back. They'd find me for sure, especially with Alissa's hard-nosed determination.

I came to the source of the wall's glow and

realized it was a door. Crouching just below the window, I listened. Satisfied that no one was on the other side, I stood and peeked through the window. The room housed monitors, displaying cameras trained on various places — building entrances, alleyways, intersections, rooms and hallways. One familiar angle, pointing at two dumpsters, caught my attention. As I examined it closely, I realized with a sinking feeling that Alissa and I had been spotted a long time ago. The mobile dumpster had been rolled away, revealing the storm grate. Alissa was nowhere in sight.

I grabbed the handle of the control room and pulled. Unlike the rest of the levers and handles in the secret tunnel, this one easily opened. Whoever installed this door must have figured they didn't need as much security if a person made it this far into the tunnel. Now in the room, I had a better view of all the monitors. From the description Alissa and Janice had given, I recognized one monitor surveyed the oak walls and mounted lamps of the off-site building belonging to The Genesee. I also got a better look at what appeared to be an interrogation room in this cluster of monitors. Whatever these people were up to, it had to be big. I took out my camera and captured a few shots of the monitors and controls. Putting the camera back in the bag, I made a mental note to take a picture of the entrance. I still had to understand the impact of this organization's surveillance around the city.

Another monitor was trained on a parking lot. There I spotted a familiar Mercedes, though I couldn't tell for certain if it belonged to Moss.

Then I spotted the Lexus, which I immediately recognized as Mr. Maddox's car. Movement in another camera caught my eye. Alissa darted down a side street. From what I could tell, she was nowhere near the storm grate we'd found. She disappeared out of view. For a second, my eyes danced from one monitor to another until I spotted her again. Someone was chasing her. In another monitor, I spotted the Jeep. It pulled up to a curb and the side door popped open. In another instant, Alissa appeared on screen. She jumped in the back seat of the Jeep. Nate took off the moment she slammed the door shut.

I placed my hands on the counter in front of me, steadying my breath and heart rate. Then on screen in my direction appeared another individual, with a full mask and cold, piercing eyes that seemed to peer right at me through the camera and onto the monitor. Whoever the person was, I felt exposed. I realized then we were in an unknown enemy's territory, looking for some evidence of wrongdoing.

Just then, I became aware of a heaviness in the room. How long it was there I didn't know. Mentally, I kicked myself for having let my guard down. I gripped the tactical pen in case I needed to strike at a pressure point. I turned into the darkness to face my unwelcome guest.

As I turned, I caught a sharp elbow to the jaw. Someone wrestled me to the ground and slammed my hand against the concrete flooring. I screamed and released my grip on the tactical pen. As I struggled to pull myself out from under the assailant's weight, the person maneuvered behind me and wrapped me in a chokehold. My vision blurred and then the room went dark.

Chapter Twenty-Nine

Alissa

As I ran, one thought seemed to pound in my head with every footfall. We'd been found. I didn't know how but someone must've been onto us since the very beginning. As I passed through the alleyway, I toppled trash cans, carts, and whatever I could to slow down whoever was in pursuit. From their footfalls, I could tell they were far enough behind me that they couldn't jump out of nowhere and tackle me. If only I could lose the person, I'd be safe. I grabbed the walkie and tapped the talk button.

"Meet me at the corner of Main and Congress," I said.

I stuffed the walkie back in my coat pocket without waiting for confirmation. Nate and Janice would know we were in big trouble. Now,

I would have to let them know someone didn't like that Marcus and I had uncovered the secret passageway. If the pursuer had found me out here, then I was sure someone found Marcus snooping down there.

Marcus, please be okay, I thought. I sent up prayers, wishing for Marcus' safety.

As I ran, I grabbed hold of a trash can, flinging it and sending it clanking across the concrete. A clank and thud followed by a curse indicated whoever was after me had fallen for my obstacle. What Cassie Maddox expected us to find, I didn't know. But I did know she had a verbal assault, coming from me, when we met again.

Just ahead, I heard the distinct roar of the Jeep. My energy went up as I moved faster. In 50 yards, I'd be home free.

Suddenly, my pursuers footfalls were closer than before. I felt a tug at my coat, but I managed to break free. The person breathed heavily, and I could tell it was a man. He sounded winded, but he had the advantage of a longer stride.

Up ahead, I could see the Jeep. The passenger door flung wide open, with Janice's wide eyes projecting enough fear and urgency for the both of us. I had to get rid of this guy because he wasn't about to go in the Jeep with us. Urging what little skill I'd gained from track and field in P.E., I took a flying leap over two trash cans already toppled over. As I sailed through the air, my pursuer stumbled and cursed. Once my feet hit the ground again, I continued to run to the Jeep. In the distance, Janice outstretched her arms.

"Hurry!" she shouted. "You're almost there.

Don't let him get you!"

Kicking it into high gear for one final sprint, I reached out and took hold of her hands. Janice grabbed me and yanked me onto the leather seats. The Jeep roared forward, and I slammed the door shut.

I wanted to be relieved, but I wasn't. I frantically looked to the front passenger's side.

"Where's Marcus?" I asked.

"We lost him just before you called," said Nate as he continued to look forward.

"We've got to find him!" I cried.

"Lis, he'll be okay," Janice said softly. "Right now, we need to go."

"We need to call for help," Nate said. "I don't know how we're going to explain all this. Let's just drive. Buckle up back there."

Once Janice and I snapped our seat belts, Nate hit the gas. The Jeep launched down several streets while hugging turns at dangerously high speeds that caused Janice and me to grip the door handles.

"Nate, slow down!" Janice yelled.

"No can do," Nate said. "We need to crack this case before it's too late."

"Don't say that," I whined.

"I'm sorry, Alissa," Nate said. "I didn't mean to upset you. We all want Marcus back. We just need to head in a direction where we think he might be."

A few choice words came to my mind until an alert pinged on someone's phone. Janice picked up her phone.

"It's Marcus!" she cheered. "His GPS tracker is

moving."

"Where is he?" I asked.

Janice pointed. "Up ahead. He's moving slowly, but he should be right around the corner of that building over there.

"Alissa, stay in the Jeep," Nate said.

Before I could protest, Nate eased on the gas and turned off the headlights. He brought the Jeep to a crawling, slow speed.

I unbuckled my seatbelt and shifted to the center of the seat to get a better view. As the Jeep moved forward, I viewed the chain-link fence of The Genesee's parking lot and off-site building.

The side door of the building opened, and two familiar people stumbled out.

"That's Marcus and Cassie!" I shouted.

Although I didn't care about Cassie, I was happy to see Marcus. I smiled, but then my smile waned. Cassie had Marcus' arm over her shoulder as she supported his weight. He appeared to limp.

"He's hurt," I said.

"Lis, let's think this through," Janice said. "We need to—"

"I don't care. I'm going after him." I squeezed the handle and pushed the door open. No one was about to tell me what to do. Not now. I stepped out and ran toward the pair. My breath quickened as I came closer. Marcus looked up.

"Lis, you're here," he said. As he let go of Cassie, he stumbled, but I caught him.

"I'm never letting you go," I whispered. I pulled him to me.

"Sorry, but you're gonna have to let go at some point," Cassie said.

My nostrils flared. I was ready to curse Cassie out, and that wasn't my style. I turned to her, but my expression changed when I noticed she held a package.

"I know you probably hate my guts, but you guys are gonna want to get out of here fast," she said.

I nodded. She was lucky I couldn't tell her what I was thinking. Getting Marcus back to safety was more important.

"Let's get you to the Jeep," I said. I wrapped his arm around my shoulders.

Behind us, I heard commotion. Marcus picked up the pace. Together we did our best to run. We were going to make it. We had to make it.

Janice popped her door open and slid over. Marcus and I scrambled into the Jeep. Once I slammed the door shut, we took off.

"Is he okay?" Janice asked. "What happened in there?"

"Someone caught me off guard and knocked me out," Marcus mumbled. "Next thing I knew I woke up in total darkness. Then Cassie came and untied me."

He closed his eyes and leaned back. Janice and I looked out the back window. If we were being followed, no one appeared to be on the road.

"Let's just get home," I said. "Tomorrow is still a school day and we don't have much sleep ahead of us."

"She played us," Nate said. "And I'm pretty sure she's been playing us this whole time."

Ignoring Nate's comments, I snuggled closer to Marcus and closed my eyes. Whatever Cassie was up to, and whatever we'd uncovered would have to wait until tomorrow.

Chapter Thirty

Marcus

The next morning, I ran the two miles to school.

According to Mom, Dad had decided to let me sleep. Then she went into a barrage of questions about whether I was on something. She didn't know the half of it. I still felt a little groggy from the night before, though I couldn't even begin to explain how I'd gotten home. One moment I was struggling with some guy on the floor. Then in the next moment, Cassie was untying me and slapping me awake. I had a fleeting memory of Alissa snuggling up to me, but I don't remember what my parents talked about when we'd gotten home. I also imagined Cassie and her father, this Detective Maddox, would have some words, too, and maybe a few laughs about how we'd been led on. I also wondered what take Alissa, Janice, and

Nate would have on last night's adventure.

When I arrived at school, the front secretary buzzed me in. Dad and Moss stepped into the office.

"There's a model student for you," Principal Moss said sarcastically. "Guess being the kid of an administrator doesn't get you very far."

"I can handle my son," Dad said sternly. "Now if you'll excuse me, I plan to have a word in private." Dad gestured to me. "This way, Marcus."

Principal Moss glared at me as I joined Dad in his office. Dad shut the door and indicated that I should take a seat.

Taking in a few deep breaths, Dad studied me. From the clothes I wore last night and my mop of knotted hair, I realized I was probably in no condition to go to school today.

"What you and your team did last night was reckless," Dad said.

"Dad, we were—"

"Careful, right?" Dad asked as he cut me off. He leaned in. "I shouldn't know this, nor should you, but whatever you guys were up to set up a lot of alarms down at the police station."

I sat up. "Really?"

"Don't look so happy about it. You four are barely amateur sleuths. But you're observant and seem to be very good at finding things out." Dad sat back. "Still, you shouldn't be out investigating...criminal cases. That's a job for adults."

"Okay," I said as I stood. "What did you find?"

"Watch it, son," Dad said. He opened the door.

"That discussion will have to wait. Off to class you go."

Dad practically pushed me out of his office, giving me no other option but to do as he said. When I passed through the office, Principal Moss's glaring expression welcomed me once again. Entering the hallway to head to class, I wondered what this guy knew that I didn't. I also wondered if Dad and this Detective Maddox knew that Moss was there last night.

Despite the swarm of activity around us, Alissa, Janice, Nate and I sat at the lunch table, picking at our food. Alissa put her fork down and pushed away her tray.

"I can't do this," she said.

"What are you talking about?" I asked.

She flailed her arms in the air. "I can't do this fake stuff. We're all just sitting around like the case is over. Let's start with Cassie. Where'd she find you anyway?"

I shrugged. "I have no idea. Between being shrouded in darkness and tied up, I didn't have much time to get a look at the place."

"C'mon, Marc! You must've seen something. Was it a storage closet or an interrogation room?"

"He did come out the off-site building," Janice added. "He must've been in the same room Mel and Abby were in."

"Did someone call me?" asked Mel. She slid over to our table. "I don't know what's got you all worked up, but you're talking about me."

"Go you," Nate said flatly. He turned away from her.

"Ooh," Mel said jokingly. "Someone's in a sour mood."

"Mel, don't mind him," Janice said. "We didn't get much sleep."

"I can see that," Mel said. "You all look like the walking dead, especially Marcus here." She gave me a once-over. "What did you do, sleep in your clothes last night?"

"As a matter of fact, I did," I replied. I sat up straighter. "And I'm proud of it."

"Don't mind the boys, Mel," said Alissa. "They're just kidding." Alissa looked around. "Where's Abby?"

Mel shrugged. "I have no idea. We're not tied to the hip and we really only hang out at school and lacrosse. Still, there's something else." Mel lowered her voice. "You all set off alarms at the country club."

Alissa's face went red. "I don't suppose your chauffer noticed."

Mel shook her head. "He didn't. I called my friend to take care of it. She's pretty good."

"Would your friend happen to be Cassie Maddox?" I asked curiously.

"I think you're right, Marc," Alissa said snidely. "Mel's friends with Cassie Maddox, the girl that spoofed my Instagram account and met up with my boyfriend."

"Yup, all that's true," Mel said anxiously. "But it doesn't matter. You guys passed the test. You're officially the good guys. Yay!" She cleared her throat. "But seriously, you're on the in now."

"That's not enough," I said. "I need to know who Cassie Maddox is. I'm tired of getting the runaround."

"Right," Mel said. "She's a private investigator. Sometimes, her father outsources cases to her, but mostly she works on her own. She's sort of like you guys except she does it legally."

"Hey," Nate said as he turned to Mel. "We do things legal...ish."

I thought about how Cassie was able to find me. No way was I going to believe she did that legally. A quick glance at the blank faces of the others told me they didn't buy it "Okay, Mel, you've got us," I said. "Who else is looped in on this case?"

"No one," Mel said. "Abby definitely doesn't know. Neither do those who are benefiting from this little racket they are playing." She slapped a hand over her mouth and her face held a bewildered expression. Her wide eyes gazing back at us.

"Cat's out of the bag," Janice said knowingly.

Mel groaned. "Just don't tell anyone, okay?"

"We won't," Alissa said. "How about adults. Do any other adults besides your parents and the authorities know anything about this case?"

"Not that I know of," Mel said. "Cassie and her father have only told me what they thought I needed to know."

"Fine," Nate said. "All this is just fine. But why are you telling us this now?"

Mel stood. "Because it isn't over. I'm pretty sure they're going to use you for the next phase. But don't ask me how." Mel looked to Alissa. "See ya in class, girl."

We watched as Mel walked off. As she exited the cafeteria and passed us in the hallway on the other side of the wall of glass, she didn't bother to check our reaction.

"I don't know, guys," Alissa said. "Mel sounded pretty confident that whatever these people had on her had been taken care off. I think it has something to do with that package Cassie had in her hand last night. I saw it when I grabbed Marcus. I'm pretty sure we were baited into going there."

"You got that right!" Nate said as he tapped his hand on the table "I've been beating myself up over it since she revealed herself last night."

The bell rang and I slowly rose from the table. The rest of the crew gathered trash as we prepared to go to class.

"I vote we let this thing rest tonight," I said. "I'm beat."

"I second that," Janice said.

Nate and Alissa seemed to stare each other down.

"Is there a problem?" I asked.

"No, we're good," Nate said. "But I'm telling you now that if something comes up tonight, I'm jumping at it."

"Me, too," Alissa said.

"Okay," I said as I rolled my eyes. "I'm headed to class."

"I'll walk with you," Alissa said.

After dumping our trays, we walked side by side through the busy hallway.

"That was new," I said. "You and Nate never see eye-to-eye. I think I witnessed history just now."

Alissa hooked her arm in mine. "Guess there's a first time for everything."

I chuckled. "I guess there is."

When we parted ways, I couldn't help but realize how much working on these cases had pulled us together. As I stepped into my next class, I knew I couldn't pass up on whatever the next phase of this case would be. I only hoped it wouldn't be nearly as risky as it was earlier this morning.

Chapter Thirty-One

Alissa

"Did you say something?" asked my coworker.

"Nope," I lied, removing my hand from my ear.

While my coworker, a teen like me, went to another table, I caught my breath. We had officially made it into the Genesee. I drew my attention to Miguel, the waiter staff supervisor. While he spoke, I exchanged a quick glance with Mel and Janice, both of whom didn't so much as flinch when Detective Maddox's voice came over the coms. Along with some pros, we were his team's eyes and ears.

"All right gang," Miguel said. "Remember, as always to keep the drinks fresh and the hors d'oeuvres coming. When it's time for the main event, keep yourselves as inconspicuous as possible."

His eyes seemed to rest on me. Apparently, Miguel had been working this place as Detective Maddox's inside guy. What he knew, I sure wanted to know. With less than a few hours of training, I was still giddy with the idea of being placed here, inside The Genesee, on a real sting operation.

"You need to get close enough to our targets for your mic to pick up on their chatter," said Detective Maddox over my earpiece.

When Miguel dismissed us, we turned and received the first tray handed to us. Mine was filled with what looked like fried calamari. I did not like calamari.

"Lis," Mel whispered to me as she passed. "Play it cool. You are looking way too obvious."

"Is this better?" I asked. I swallowed back disgust and put on a bright smile.

"Just c'mon," Mel said.

I stepped aside as she balanced a tray in one hand and pushed through the right side of the swinging double doors. Janice approached, her head held high and her tray precariously balanced in one hand outstretched in front of her. I held back a chuckle as I followed her out the door.

Patrons milled about in small groups, attempting to one up each other in pompous talk about their stock holdings or their child's latest achievements. When I stopped at each group, their chatter ceased as each patron reached for what my platter held.

"I love calamari!" a woman exclaimed. She grabbed a morsel off my plate, downed it, and reached for another. "Do you mind?"

"Sure," I said. I held the platter closer to her. "Enjoy."

I watched as the woman scarfed down another piece, and I couldn't help but feel disgusted again. I know I typically wouldn't be able to get into a country club, but I expected the patrons to have better manners. When the woman gulped her last bit of champagne, I quickly left the table.

As I raised my platter once more, I caught sight of Miguel. With a nod, he gestured me to move along.

So, the time went, though with far less dramatics. I seemed to float from one cluster of patrons to another. When the platter was empty, I returned to the kitchen for a replacement. I sat my plate down and turned.

"Whoa!" Janice exclaimed as she pulled her platter out of the way. "We nearly decorated you with crab and cheese dip."

"Close call," I said as I laughed. "Better get going."

Miguel handed me a platter, containing an assortment of cheese and crackers.

"Make your way over to table ten," he said.

I nodded. He wanted us rotating throughout the dining hall, so groups would not be immediately bombarded with another tray before they could finish what they'd taken. There was another reason, too. Detective Maddox wanted a 360-degree audio of the place. Once again laden with a platter of hors d'oeuvres balanced in one hand, I placed my free hand on the door and glided back into the dining hall. As I did so, I wondered where Alfred Maddox, the club's president was holed up. I glanced around. Perhaps, he was entertaining the guest of honor, whoever that was.

"Excuse me, miss," a female voice called.

I stopped and turned. An elegantly dressed woman, standing between two handsome middle-aged men, waited for me. As I approached her group, her smile faded.

"I know you," she said. "You're at Lenape High."

I nodded and offered her the platter. As she and her entourage took a sampling, it was then I recognized the new head guidance counselor Ms. Calhoun. I made my way toward table ten to stop at a few small groups. When I did, I caught a glance of Ms. Calhoun out of the corner of my eye. Each time I did, her eyes met mine. I had a feeling she suspected me.

Coming to table ten, I spotted two families. Like the other men, the fathers wore tuxedoes, while the women wore evening gowns. While I'm not much for fashion, something about these women made them seem more finely dressed. Their children, two teenagers, sat with their back to me, apparently laughing right alongside their parents. As I approached the table, I caught snippets of conversation.

"Well," one mother bragged. "My daughter has been accepted for their crew team," she said. "Can you believe it? She's never been on a...what do you call it? A canoe! That's it."

Her husband leaned in and whispered something in her ear. Red faced, she made eye contact with me.

"Well, come along, dear," said the woman. "You're not paid to stand there and look pretty."

As one of the teenagers turned, I immediately found myself gazing at Abby Jenkins. She froze.

"Excuse me for a second," Abby said. "I'm going to make a special request."

Her mother waved her off as Abby took me gently by the arm, leading me away.

"What are you doing here?" she asked in a huff.

"I'm working, duh," I said.

"You just can't be here. Whatever this is. It's bad."

I scoffed. "Can you stop pretending? Just tell me already. Did you seriously get on Penamore's crew team?"

Abby laughed. "No, the other girl did, though. Why? What's this about?"

Over my com, I heard Detective Maddox's voice crackle. "Your cover's blown. Find a way out of there."

"Excuse me," I said.

Abby held my arm tighter. "You're working. I need you to get me out of here before it starts?"

"What are you talking about?" I asked.

The rhythmic chiming of fine silverware on half-empty wine glasses began to fill the dining hall. Clusters of adults broke in unison, regrouping at their tables like a well-choreographed dance. I realized then that I was the only server still on the floor.

"Abby, I need to go," I whispered. "What's going on?"

"C'mon," she said. "I need to get out of here,

too."

In the front of the room, stage lights flickered on as the dining hall dimmed. As Abby dragged me to the back of the room and further from the stage, a microphone buzzed.

"And now, ladies and gentlemen," a voice boomed from a microphone. "Before the main course, I'd like to introduce to you our guest of honor..."

I glanced over my shoulder to spot Mr. Maddox, spouting various accolades for someone everyone apparently already knew.

"Abby, wait!" I yelled as I pulled away from her. When I got out of her grasp, the tray clattered to the floor. Cheese and crackers scattered across the floor.

In mid-sentence, Alfred Maddox paused.

"Excuse me, miss," he said. "You shouldn't be here. Would someone escort this young lady out?"

All eyes seemed to be on me as two well-dressed men with noticeable wired mics attached to their ears approached me in long strides.

"What part of get out do you not understand?" asked Detective Maddox as his voice crackled in my ear.

I ran to the door. The men were upon me, and so were the eyes of every guest in the room. The door wouldn't budge. Furniture seemed to shuffle with nervous energy. I pushed again. On either side of me, Genesee security grabbed my arms.

The microphone boomed once again, but this time with a familiar voice.

"It's okay," Principal Moss said. "I know her.

She's one of mine at Lenape High."

I relaxed a little. Moss was here to bail me out. I never thought I'd be happy to see him, but I was. The men on either side of me loosened their grip as they faced Moss, his figure still and imposing in the stage lights.

"Still," Principal Moss said. "She shouldn't be here."

Beside me, Abby seemed to fade into the darkness of the room.

Just then the doors opened toward me. I spun out of the loosened grip of Genesee security and darted through the door. I was in such a hurry that I didn't watch where I was going. I collided with another group of people, but this time I felt relieved. Detective Maddox, surrounded by an armed police force, smiled down at me.

"Erikson, please see this young lady makes it out the door," said Detective Maddox.

Erikson, a uniformed officer, obliged. As I followed him out the door, Detective Maddox stepped forward.

"This is Lenape County Sherriff's department," he said. "We have here several arrest warrants. If you nice folks can calmly take a seat, we have the entire building surrounded."

As exciting as all that sounded, I redoubled my stride. I needed to be with my parents, with my friends, and with Marcus. This, I realized was a job for the professionals.

Chapter Thirty-Two

Marcus

"I still can't believe you didn't stay for the arrest," Nate said, pouting as he took a seat beside us at lunch.

Nate had been going on like that almost every day for over a month. Since that time, Principal Moss had been arrested. Apparently, the rumors were true. He did own a Lamborghini and my dad, now the acting head Principal did find plans in Moss' office for a Jacuzzi installation in the private bathroom of the principal's office. Ms. Calhoun also quietly resigned. Rumors swirled that she'd been fixing some test scores for Alfred Maddox just in case the little admissions scam ever came under scrutiny. But that was speculation and hearsay at best. I hadn't heard anything about Cassie Maddox either, so I figured she could be on our side. I was just glad we got through the case.

Janice snuggled up next to Nate.

"Beau, let it rest," she said. "We'll have plenty of opportunities on our next case."

"Our next case," Alissa repeated. "I like the sound of that." She looked to me. "Marc, please tell me we have another case lined up." She bit her lip.

I hated when she made that face because I found her so cute. Still, I had to be honest with her.

"Sorry, babe," I said. "No case yet."

Mel joined us at the table, and so did Abby.

"Seriously," Abby said. "You guys are thrill junkies. I'm just glad you were able to get me out of going to that stupid Penamore. Sorry, Mel, no offense."

"None taken," Mel said. "I knew you'd be miserable there taking all those pre-law courses. Besides, cricket is definitely not your thing."

"Oh, please, I would've nailed it. But you're right. I'm more into beauty, so it's cosmetology school all the way." She pulled out an envelope. "Can you believe I got accepted into Paul Mitchell? I know what you're all thinking." She paused and smiled. "It's legit. They absolutely loved my portfolio."

"I knew they would," Janice said. "We're great models."

I glanced at Alissa, and even she beamed with pride. I did, too. I enjoyed getting a sneak peek at potential prom outfits as, one after another, she had shown me glamour photos, complimentary of

Abby Jenkins.

"I don't know about you all," I said. "But I can use a little break from our little escapades into the dark underworld of the shady college admissions process."

Derrick and Trey slid their trays onto the table beside us and sat.

"You're not going to take a break," Derrick said. "But I'm pretty sure you've tapped the school out."

"Why's that?" I asked.

"If you haven't noticed," Derrick said. "we're the only ones who will sit with you four."

"That's because no one will sit with you," Nate said.

"True," Derrick said. He gave us fist bumps along with Trey while the girls continued to talk about cosmetology.

"I still don't get one thing," I said.

"What's that?" Derrick asked.

"Someone slipped five test papers in my binder a while back."

Trey choked back some milk. "Sorry, that was me. I swiped them when Calhoun dropped them outside of the building."

All of us looked at him expectantly.

"What?" Trey asked. "I was just trying to help. Calhoun was dirty from the start. Besides, I knew you'd get them to your pops."

"You know he's right," Derrick said.

"That was slick, but not the most effective move," Nate said. He shook his head. "You want to know what I would have done?"

Nate didn't even wait for us to confirm our

interest as he rambled on about how he would've held out until an opportune time to use evidence of test tampering against her.

Alissa and I looked at each other knowingly. Half the time, Nate's little plans were almost always shady, but this one ranked in the top ten.

When the bell rang, our little band gathered up our things. After throwing away our trash, Alissa hooked her arm into mine.

"You know what all this means, right?" she asked.

"What's that?" I asked.

"When our next case presents itself, we'll have eyes and ears almost everywhere."

I laughed. Surely there'd be a next case. Alissa and I would take lead, and we'd reign Nate in a little. We'd work smarter. We would have to, and with the skills we'd acquired, we wouldn't make the mistake of trusting strangers, even if they turned out to be professionals like Cassie Maddox.

Coming March 2025:

Shadows of Deceit: A Cassie Maddox Mystery

In the gritty streets of Lenape City, PI Cassie Maddox uncovers a sinister web of corruption and betrayal that threatens everything she holds dear. What begins as a routine assignment quickly spirals into a deadly situation. Will Cassie Maddox summon the courage and cunning to bring justice to Lenape City, or will the shadows consume her?

https://www.indiesunited.net/shadows-of-deceit

Thanks for Reading

Thank you for taking the time to read *Operation Varsity Blues*. If you enjoyed this book, please leave a review.

https://www.goodreads.com/book/show/57970939-operation-varsity-blues

Then check out the rest of the books in the series.

A Kahale and Claude Mystery

Buy now from your favorite retailer, or visit
www.indiesunited.net/timothy-baldwin

About the Author

Tim, a seasoned educator with over 15 years of teaching experience across multiple grade levels in English and Drama, has established himself as a dedicated writer with a diverse academic background. He holds a B.S. in Theatre from Towson University, an M.A.T. from Notre Dame of Maryland University, and an M.A. in Creative Writing and Literature from Fairleigh Dickinson University.

Originally from Syracuse, New York, Tim currently resides in Maryland, where he imparts his passion for English, Creative Writing, Film, and Theatre to high school students. His journey into writing began earnestly in 2014, spurred by the encouragement of his own students.

Tim's love for storytelling stems from his upbringing, where his mother's dedication to reading to him and his siblings laid the foundation for his literary pursuits. Tim embarked on his writing endeavors, influenced by authors such as C. S. Lewis, J. R. R. Tolkien, Piers Anthony, and others in the mystery, thriller, and fantasy genres.

Since his debut publication in 2019, Tim has rapidly expanded his literary footprint, amassing a wealth of published works. Beyond writing, Tim enjoys indulging in his diverse interests, including reading, teaching, camping, savoring cigars, shooting, and attending live music concerts.

Visit Tim on the Web

www.timothyrbaldwin.com
facebook.com/timothyrbaldwin
Twitter @timothyrbaldwin
Instagram @timothyrbaldwin